Priestess of the Damned

VIRGINIA COFFMAN

PINNACLE BOOKS   LOS ANGELES

PRIESTESS OF THE DAMNED

Copyright © 1970 by Virginia Coffman

All rights reserved

A Pinnacle Books edition, published by special arrangement with the author's agent.
All rights reserved, which includes the right to reproduce this book or portions thereof in any form whatsoever. For information address:

>Jay Garon-Brooke Associates
>415 Central Park West, 17D
>New York, N.Y. 10025

ISBN: 0-52340-137-X

First printing, November 1977

Cover illustration by Bruce Minney

Printed in the United States of America

PINNACLE BOOKS, INC.
One Century Plaza
2029 Century Park East
Los Angeles, California 90067

An offering to the Powers of Darkness . . .

Once, when the spell threatened to break, Marc Meridon himself appeared unexpectedly. She recognized him by the few words he spoke, although he had not removed his hood.

At a signal the worshippers came to their feet. Spherical lights from the beamed ceiling flashed and reflected myriad colors from their many mirrored surfaces. When these effects were at their peak, Nadine raised her arms and two robed and hooded adherents bounded swiftly onto the dais, bearing between them the supple body of the blonde girl whose flesh gleamed, sometimes pink and sometimes gold, under the transparent black chiffon covering thrown over her.

She was laid upon the altar, her hair hanging over the side like a thin yellow waterfall. The girl was not drugged; the lights and the scene itself were effective enough to subdue her, and to produce the most erotic invitation in her body as it lay quietly while the Powers of Darkness were invoked over her erect breasts and ready flanks . . .

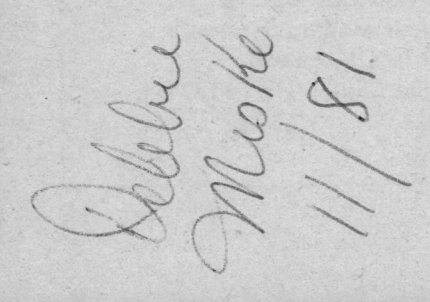

Pinnacle Books by Virginia Coffman:

THE DEVIL'S MISTRESS
PRIESTESS OF THE DAMNED

WRITE FOR OUR FREE CATALOG

If there is a Pinnacle Book you want but can't find locally, it is available from us—simply send the title and price plus 25¢ to cover mailing and handling costs to:

PINNACLE BOOKS
Reader Mailing Service
P.O. Box 1050
Rockville Centre, N.Y. 11571

___Check here if you want to receive our catalog regularly.

to Matty Monjar,
loving and giving

**PRIESTESS
OF THE
DAMNED**

ONE

Nadine Janos, striding along the mirrored foyer on her way into the hotel's Cafe Madrigal, slowed her rapid progress long enough to check all her equipment. Long before she was anybody at all in the Satan Worship Racket of San Francisco, Nadine had learned to make the best of a very meagre original endowment.

The mousy blonde hair of her youth had done nothing for a pallid complexion, but when tinted to a glossy cap of blue-black, it gave her slightly prominent blue eyes a look of remarkable hypnotic power which had a sensual effect on the beholder. Once she discovered her power, the rest was inevitable for an ambitious girl who had known poverty. She dressed up to the most striking advantage—her rather small, scrawny figure now became "svelte," "sleek," and "utterly marvelous."

On the spring night when Nadine arrived at the restaurant to meet Sean O'Flannery, her one-man Guard of Janissaries, she checked as always this carefully contrived appearance of hers. At twenty-eight she had parlayed a sharp brain plus imagination and attention to detail into a financial success that supported herself and, at a suitable distance, her feckless father and three equally feckless brothers.

Her floor-length gown tonight was of stark, Satanic black and white, the black satin tubular skirt topped by a "Thirties" white satin halter-bodice decorated by zig-zag lightning flashes of sequinned black. She might not be a beauty, but when she moved on, to stand briefly in the doorway of the hotel's elegant, shadowed cafe, she aroused the excited gasps of those groups seated at the black banquettes. Since she was a realist, all this amused Nadine and she was smiling a bit cynically, in spite of her present business worries, when the handsome young maitre d' hurried over to greet her.

"Miss Janos! How good to see you again! The Irish gentleman has already arrived. He is at your table."

"Good. In his racket he doesn't have to create an entrance." She winked at the young Frenchman whose dignity and carefully romantic appearance did not permit him to wink back. But he also forebore asking the obvious question— What, precisely, was O'Flannery's racket? The rugged, attractive fellow drank a lot, occasionally devoured a rare steak, was always on hand when Miss Janos needed him, and otherwise seemed to subsist on her handouts. It was perfectly well known at the Madrigal and elsewhere that Miss Janos footed all the bills. No one had ever seen O'Flannery produce so much as a dime. Still, the young maitre d' thought, watching Nadine make her way to the banquette just ahead of him, rather than behind, the Irishman undoubtedly had his uses.

O'Flannery did not rise until Nadine was being seated beside him, and then he untangled his legs only long enough to make the expected gesture, no more. He seemed reasonably sober to Nadine's quick eye, but then, he seldom seemed otherwise. She often thought she despised him. He let himself be used by her, twisted around her small, thin fingers so easily. He knew her, down to her very vitals, and still he loved her. He was either a fool or an angel, or something of both, she decided.

She had never asked herself what her life would be like without him. It was a contingency so remote as to be almost non-existent. She leaned over and brushed his cheek lightly with a kiss before letting him take her free hand as she balanced the big parchment menu with the other.

"Did you find out anything about our Mystery Man?" he asked finally as she was debating between the Poached Salmon Madrigal and the Noisette of Lamb. She was careful to give her order, along with a Vodka-on-the-Rocks before she seemed to put her attention to his remark.

Then she murmured dramatically, "Take it easy, Friend. Even the walls have ears." Although she intended this as a joke, there was a special, wry flavor to it, and they both recognized the fact. Nadine glanced around the room, whose gold, black and white elegance was barely illuminated by crystal decorated sconces. She shivered and O'Flannery asked.

"Cold, Princess? Did you check your jacket?"

She said unnecessarily, "It's not that," and they looked at each other. A wordless, chilling idea had begun to obsess them recently about the manager-owner of the exclusive Spa down the California Coast at Lucifer Cove. Nadine had been operating her Devil's Coven there for several months with great success, but more and more, she was aware of practical outside influences, and she couldn't decide whether these influences were meant to help or to hinder her. She wanted no partners in her undertaking, no moneyed backers. She worked alone. She hated interference. She needed only O'Flannery. And any other man or woman who tried to lend assistance, financial or otherwise in order to get into the act, was instantly booted out. This was the one subject from which the Irishman could not protect her, and there were moments when she showed an uncharacteristic concern about it.

"You made the calls? And the locals, these San Franciscans what do they say about him?"

The big glass was set before her with its unneeded black swizzle stick, and she took a long drink before playing the stick around through the holes in the ice cubes, and then taking another drink.

"Here, girl, easy . . . easy." O'Flannery protested, one of those bits of advice that always sounded odd, coming from him. When she ignored him, he reached over and slid the glass neatly out of her fingers.

She scowled. "Irish, don't get me started."

"I hope you won't. Now, if you'll be simmering down and getting to the nitty-gritty! I suppose they all gave you negative reports. He interferes in business, he cuts out the competition, he's fruity, he's a woman-chaser, he's Mafia . . ."

Nadine tried to get over his hand to fool with the swizzle stick and he gave her that, alone and dripping. She sucked on the ball at the end of the stick. "No. None of it."

"No habits, good or bad? Impossible. Then it's purely money. He owns Lucifer Cove and he's angling to get a kickback from you. How about wills and bequests? Maybe he wants a piece of that action. Your little Devil Lovers Anonymous had two deaths in the last month. He probably figures to play on that."

"You just don't get the picture." She looked up at him suddenly, her blue eyes wondering, seeking an assurance he couldn't give her. "Marc Meridon isn't talked about."

"They don't know him. Well, we always thought he came from Europe."

"He isn't talked about. They know him. But they get shifty-eyed, and shifty-tongued, too. It's weird. The whole thing is just one big hush-hush bit. Even the ancient seadog who runs the Forty-Niner Packing Corporation gave me the same idiot stare. It's the same with everybody who's made it big in this town. Everybody I talked to."

"Maybe they really don't know Meridon."

"Oh, come off it, Irish! Don't you remember Meridon in the Cove at Christie Deeth's cocktail party the other night? Someone asked him if he did much sailing. He made that joke about teaching Old Man Haggedorf how to sail deep-water ships." She laughed. "And that would take some doing. Haggedorf is in his eighties and Marc Meridon must be ten years younger than—" She did not finish but what she had not said was obvious.

"Younger than me?" he finished pleasantly. "Well, he doesn't look over thirty. I'll give him that. But then," his grin was twisted as always, "I've had a hard life."

She said "Ha!" with not quite the ridicule his remark deserved. Then the first course of her dinner arrived and she began to eat while O'Flannery ordered another Rye with water chaser. She had given up worrying about his liquid diet.

By the time she had silently worried her way through dinner to the dessert, she was feeling a little more optimistic. A childhood conspicuously devoid of such luxury sweets as the Dobishertorte she was now eating, gave them a special curative power on her nerves. O'Flannery had begun on a steak so rare it was barely dead. There were no "trimmings" of potatoes or vegetables to take room away from his serious eating and drinking. Being used to all this, Nadine ignored his effort to eat in peace and laid out her problems, more to hear them herself than to get an immediate solution. The Cafe Madrigal had filled by now, and the buzz of conversation, plus the pleasant, nerve-soothing music piped in, helped to cover her low-pitched voice, trained though it was to be heard as "Devil's High Priestess" amid the bad acoustics of private halls.

"When we went into Lucifer Cove we had no trouble at all getting the loan to equip that little temple with stereo for our ceremonies. And the trick lighting, and all the trappings. It was just the way that idiotic old cultist, Edna Schallert, predicted it would be. Okay, I'll buy the fact that the Cove was a natural for my kind of game, but the bank didn't know what my business was. All those super-rich old bags and the ancient, impotent males, I suppose they were just panting a bit for the old Devil bit. They've got nowhere else to go, no other thrills left. But ever since we've been there, I've had this creepy feeling it's too easy. Like . . . some Howard Hughes'-type super-big shot wants in on the profits, and he may pull the rug out any minute."

"Have you ever considered that maybe Meridon does own the Hot Springs along with the Spa? And maybe he thinks you are good business for the Cove?" He squinted at her over a neatly cut square of dripping steak. "I wouldn't be at all surprised if your Satan gimmicks are responsible for the change in the crowd there. A lot of lookers among those females, and they're coming in with tidy portfolios of the negotiable variety."

A fierce little flicker of jealousy burned through her. "I don't doubt it. Sex is still pretty negotiable."

"But money's even better. Is that what you're thinking, Princess?" He grinned and went on chewing with great enjoyment.

All the same, she thought he was very close to correct about her. Money. Power. The theatrical glamor and the challenge of her chosen field. Surely, some day, at some unexpected hour, the bitter childhood of an unimportant, unwanted, totally ordinary little girl would be wiped out by the adult triumphs of Nadine Janos, High Priestess of the Devil, a woman never to be accounted *ordinary*, whatever else she might be.

Feeling deflated, she recognized the signs of impending trouble, one of those periodic moods that engulfed her in waves of ghastly depression.

"I've got to get back. I've been away from the temple almost—How long?" She figured rapidly. "Thirty hours. You know that motorcycle pair that killed the parents in the Bel-Air garage? They've been hanging around the temple. They may be vandals. If they burn those new Black Sabbath altar curtains, I swear I'll do what those hung juries didn't do. I'll mow them down myself. I wonder why Mr. Meridon admitted them to the Cove. They're not the kind we usually see at the Spa, not quite our—"

"Not our sort?" he asked ironically.

She started to get up. "I've got to go back in a minute." She was hauled back briefly by his firm hand pinning her wrist.

"Why?"

Indignant, she asked, *"Why do you think?"* And he let her go, but as she crossed the floor toward the hyperglamorous black and gold Ladies Room not forgetting her confident stride, she understood perfectly well what he meant. He always knew when the depression came over her and had once stalked into the Ladies Room at the Cliff House, to the horror of other patrons, and knocked half a dozen aspirins out of her hand. The idiot thought she was trying to kill herself when she was only trying to calm herself, a matter different in degree, but not, unfortunately, in kind. She was on her way now to take a couple of simple, non-prescription tranquilizers, that might, or might not, revive her inner tranquility.

What is it? she thought shakily. What am I so damned afraid of?

The investment in that beat-up little "Greek

Temple" at exclusive Lucifer Cove was an astonishing success. Up until late last year when Edna Schallert told her about the Cove, Nadine's followers had been the Far Out, the Kooks, the Jokesters. Suddenly, at the Cove, she began to promote money from the cream of an over-endowed society. So why this worry, this tight knot in her stomach, and the wave upon wave of depression? Perhaps it was the very fact that her luck had run too well, thanks in part to the good will of sombre, dark-eyed young Marc Meridon who had a financial interest in the Lucifer Cove Spa. He troubled her, especially his motives. She had never been able to accept unsolicited favors with any grace.

"Hi," said the checkroom girl, whose mini-uniform of black nylon looked strangely old-fashioned in a new, maxi-world. "Conjured up any demons lately?"

For some reason Nadine hated to have her so-called powers treated lightly, though her first defense when attacked for leading the gullible astray was that only a fool took her tricks seriously. She answered the greeting with a brief, "Busy, busy," hoping the girl hadn't seen her swallow the capsules. Next thing anybody knew, there'd be gossip about Nadine Janos being "on the stuff."

"You having dinner with Mr. Goodlooking? I saw him out there near your table."

Amused, Nadine ran a hand over her hair to smooth any rebellious tendrils into place. "Yes. I take it he drank a full meal before I arrived." Seeing the girl's reflection in the long dressing table mirror, she paused, studying the girl's blank look. "You *are* talking about Sean O'Flannery; aren't you?"

The blank look lifted to reveal little ripples of amusement. "Oh! You had me wondering. The one I'm talking about doesn't look the type. Wonderful eyes, by the way. The dark kind I could drown in. I just naturally figured he was sitting with you."

Good God! thought Nadine in an explicable panic. Meridon must be here, spying on us. I wonder if he overheard anything about our investigation, for instance ... Aloud, she said calmly, "You don't know where he sat?"

"Well, if it wasn't at your table, it had to be that one right behind you." The girl's thickly layered makeup broke into faintly oily little streaks of pleasure. "He's so gentle. Marvelous manners. And yet, you get the feeling he could be just a teensy bit ruthless, no matter how those nice big black eyes look at you. He hinted if I ever got at outs here, he might have a place for me. Is he legit?"

Nadine made light of the whole thing, "Oh, I think so" but she shivered and got up. "You may be talking about Marc Meridon. He's one of the owners at Lucifer Cove, down the Peninsula beyond Carmel."

"Aha! Where you operate," the girl said knowledgeably. "Wish I had the bread it takes to get in there. Got to remould these damned hips of mine pretty soon. Since I gave up the weed, I've eaten myself right out of my uniform."

When Nadine went back out into the restaurant, blinking at the dark punctuated by the miniscule candlelights that greeted her, she peered over the back of the banquette, finding the other side empty.

"What's the matter?" Irish wanted to know, raising a tawny eyebrow mildly. "Is the place bugged?"

"It may as well be. Irish, *he's* been here!"

He did not make the mistake of pretending to misunderstand. "Seems to be gone now. You sure it was Meridon?" She was. "Well, it's not too surprising. One of those jokers you interviewed today must have called him."

"It figures," she agreed glumly. "Let's go."

He made no objection, and having gotten her new sable jacket and thrown it around her bare shoulders, he let Nadine tip the checkroom girl, as he also let her tip the parking attendant when they went down into Union Square Garage.

"Some day," she muttered, getting behind the wheel, "I'm going to give you a fistful of bills and you're going to pay these damned characters yourself. Do you realize they all think you're a gigolo?"

He grinned, directing her out onto the busy street with sign language, and reminding her at the same time, "Gigolos are all under six feet, with olive green eyes."

That brought a laugh and Nadine's reminder, "You're showing your age, Old Boy, if that's your idea," and in better humor she drove out Geary toward the San Jose Freeway. It was difficult to remain either moody or depressed, with Irish beside her.

By midnight they were well beyond Carmel, headed along the narrow, twisting and turning coast Highway where the peculiar white light refracted from the Pacific roller helped to illuminate the ins and out of the coastal cliffs.

"Funny how noisy those waves are tonight," O'Flannery remarked, lowering the window and scowling out at the windy sea. Biting cold air with a salty tang, swirled through the car, ruffling Nadine's hair, but she bit off an irritable complaint after a glance at her companion. It was troubling to see that O'Flannery the Unflappable was not as calm as he usually appeared, and she didn't want to add to things by minor complaints.

"The noisy waves aren't the problem," she said briskly. "I've never driven the route at this hour. Can you see ahead?"

"Pretty dark. The turnoff's somewhere around here. This Golden State could afford to give us a little of that golden light along here."

"Look for Sentinel Rock. The turnoff is just behind it."

The winding road ahead had an eerie white aura, due to the way the car lights cut across the heavy curtains of coastal fog, and Nadine marveled at its ability to change all the remembered landmarks into unknown hazards. They had not passed a car in the last fifteen minutes, which was a relief in one way, because there were curves on the road that were little better than switchbacks and required a steady hand and unshakeable nerves when pot-smoking Big Sur visitors came sailing around a corner in the wrong lane, obviously primed for a head-on collision.

"Sentinel Rock coming up," O'Flannery said in a return to his calm way. He leaned forward, peering through the windshield, directing her.

"It's the biggest granite peak there beyond the light. You'll have to turn sharp. Don't forget."

Greatly relieved, as though the weight had been removed from her back and mind, Nadine turned to the left and suddenly the air was filled with explosive noises roaring and a light blazed in their faces, momentarily blinding them. Nadine screamed and swung sharply right, aided by the quick hand of O'Flannery upon the wheel. There was a crunch of metal and seconds later the world seemed to dissolve into infinite bits of light and darkness.

"You all right, Princess?" O'Flannery asked shakily. "Princess?"

Her stomach hurt as she rocked back and forth, her head was whirling, and she groped for O'Flannery's warm, hard hand, laughing hysterically. "Good old safety belt... What happened?"

"Motorcycle." Two of those kids from the Cove. No! Don't look. They've bought it. I'll handle things.

She nodded but found herself shaken into awareness by his hammering at the hood which was badly jammed. He got out and seconds later, she saw his face, pale in the remaining car light. She couldn't make out what he was looking at. Queer little puffs of either smoke or fog rose from the ground and the mass of tortured metal. She heard herself whispering "Thank God!" for the whirring noise like wheels that spun endlessly, blocking out sounds of human agony, if there was anyone alive out there. O'Flannery came around to her car window whose glass covered her lap, but barely grazed her cheek and neck.

"I can't find any life. It was those two that got

the hung juries last year. I guess the jury was still out and they didn't know it."

"Don't," the horror of the crime which the twenty-year old pair had first admitted to and then recanted—the murder of the girl's parents for her inheritance—was now blurred by their ghastly finish. Nadine thought about this, and as the night closed around them, salty, pitiless as only the indifferent can be, she cried out.

O'Flannery said, "Move over. Maybe we can back out. We've got to get to the police." She obeyed him, beginning rapidly to recover.

"Irish, I thought of something." He was busy trying to get the motor started and did not look at her. He asked absently, "What?"

"Do you suppose Meridon had something to do with this? I saw the way he was looking at those two kids yesterday at the Spa luncheon.

"So what? I wasn't fond of them either. They caused enough trouble at the Cove."

"It wasn't that. I saw the way he looked at them. Not angry. Not the way you get. But oddly. Thoughtful and sad. As if—he knew something would happen like this."

O'Flannery snorted. "In that case, I wish he'd confided in me. We nearly got ourselves killed."

"Don't you see, Irish? I *want* to believe somebody else wished this on them. Because otherwise, it's almost as if I did the wishing. As if I was responsible for their deaths. As—in a way—I guess I am. I shouldn't ever have said that about killing them."

"Princess, you're hysterical and slightly nuts."

But she wasn't. She knew she wasn't. It had been like this several months ago, Irena Byaglu, that silly cultist who had been her friend, became just too silly, demanding too many "miracles" of love from a man who couldn't return her love, and Nadine had wished the woman would stop hounding her. "Why doesn't she just up and die, if she's so damnably unhappy" was how Nadine had expressed it to herself. Or to O'Flannery? And Irena Byaglu had died. Within the next couple of days. It was uncanny. Now this.

"I wish I could blame Meridon, somehow. I wish I could blame someone else. . . . Irish, is it possible I've dabbled in this business so long I've developed some kind of gruesome power to kill people?"

"We're getting you home, Princess. Fast! You've really got 'em now. You need rest."

But what if...

She sat there sucking the cold, white knuckles of her hand, wondering.

TWO

The entire frightful business was handled with dispatch by a cruising sheriff's car which showed up like magic only minutes after O'Flannery backed out of the Cove road. He blinked the remaining car light, signalling them through the darkness and in no time the two laconic officers had managed to take over the investigation, indicating that these witnesses were unwanted and would be called on later for their reports. Meanwhile, the coroner would be notified.

"But isn't there any hope at all that they might be alive?" Nadine asked, her horror numbed by this time.

"No," said one of the hard-eyed men flatly, with the mechanical lack of expression that made the scene even less human. "The male was beheaded. The female was in nearly as bad—"

"I understand," she said faintly. "Maybe we can get on home, Irish. I feel—Never mind." He was helping the second officer examine the dreadful dark heap that had once been human flesh.

But O'Flannery was there a minute or two later, getting in behind the wheel, putting his hand out briefly to squeeze her cold fingers. "It's over, Princess. Don't think about it. You've got a show to put on tomorrow night. With all your devilish tricks. And meanwhile, you need rest and sleep."

She straightened her back, sat up, and tried to borrow some of his strength. "Thanks, Honey." Curiously enough, it was easier after that, once Irish had indicated his confidence in her ability to recover the old Nadine Janos.

She kept repeating her name, mentally. It was the charm that had worked for her from the time she was five. "Nadine Janos. I'm Nadine Janos. *They*—(The world, the individual, society, all those who humiliated or overlooked or despised her) *They don't know who I am!*" Having repeated to herself the silly phrase, she smiled faintly, felt new life surge through her, and relaxed.

They drove carefully around the point of the accident and onto the paved road which led into Lucifer Cove. At the beginning of the turnoff, the road was unobtrusive, filled with pebbles, and partially concealed by the wall of cliffs flanking the entrance. It had been suggested by the cynical that these hazards were deliberately set up by an obliging nature in order to weed out those would-be clients of the Spa who were not among the Super-Rich Beautiful People. As Nadine knew quite well, this was only a half-truth. All kinds of people came to Lucifer Cove. Some who were not super-rich, like Ricardo Shahnaz who worked as a dance instructor at the Hot Springs, simply found their proper niche.

"As I found mine," she thought with sudden distaste for the idea of being commonplace and ordinary.

Generally, Nadine had a suite at the luxurious

Spa, the most prominent building in the little valley which was bordered on three sides by the Coast Range. The Hot Springs loomed up against the north rock wall, spewing sulphur that occasionally befouled the air of the imitation-Tudor village. The tiny, white-columned Greek Temple, scene of Nadine's best priestly shows, crowned a shelf of earth and shale halfway up the south cliff. The Hot Springs site was always visible and at all hours, thanks to the ghastly, eye-watering yellow fumes that hovered over the north end of the valley. From some points of vantage it was possible to see Nadine's temple on the south, but the entrance road was so curiously constructed that it soon wandered into many roads, including village streets, concealed from each other by twisted cypress and clumps of prickly seashore plants half-dead and stained yellow from the sulphur in the ground. This tricky road often got the newcomer hopelessly lost before he, or more frequently she, reached the Spa in the village center. Another trick to discourage the unwanted newcomer? Opinions were unanimous on this, since it happened so often.

"Where to tonight?" O'Flannery asked, finding the miniature white light strung at the side of one of the intersections, and hitting the right road into the Cove's main street. "The Spa?"

She looked at him gratefully. "Thanks. But much as I'd prefer to, I've got to get up to the temple tonight. I can't stand sleeping without knowing the place is all right. I can sleep there, in the room back of the altar." At his sudden look, she added defensively. "It's quite comfortable. And it certainly won't be the first time I've spent the night there."

"Yes, but I was there too. Or have you forgotten?"

She felt her flesh faintly warm at that and was angry at her own virginal reaction to his reminder. Her life had not been crowded with lovers. In general, she achieved her ambitions by means less orthodox, her brain and her skill as a performer. But O'Flannery, who began as one of her lovers, had superseded others along the way and she was sometimes of the opinion that he alone discouraged them in mysterious ways.

"Don't be funny. Tonight's been too horrible, and I'm too tired to trade jokes."

"In that case, no point in my escorting you up the hill to the temple tonight."

He knew perfectly well she counted on his protection tonight up the trail to the temple; yet he knew also that she was too keyed up, too tense to make love on this particular night. Would he get all upset about it, accusing her of not playing the game, of being the tease, the bitch, all the things she had heard before in such tiresome detail?

"Irish..."

This time he didn't look her way. She saw from the throb of the vein over his left eyebrow that he recognized her ploy, the soft, whimsical tone, the hint of coaxing.

"So? What comes now?"

"Of course I want your help tonight. You know it. Nobody knows me the way you do." She reached out, laid her hand on his knee. "It's just that I need your help because I'm so—"

"Tired. The old, old song and dance of the old, old housewife from old, old Scarsdale."

She jerked her hand back, angry because she had predicted the whole scene, angry because, of all insults, the worst for Nadine Janos, was to be the typical, the commonplace. And he knew it.

They drove past the Spa in silence. She knew then that he was at least going to the foot of the temple path with her. Thanks for small favors, anyway!

Trying to keep her mind off the problems, imaginary and otherwise, that the ambitious scrambling of a young lifetime had developed for her, Nadine looked around at the quiet little main street of Lucifer Cove. Lined with Tudor fronts of stark black and white half-timbering, the street always gave Nadine the creepy feeling that she had stumbled into the past, a dangerous time, churning with evil. Even after ten months here she wasn't sure of what lay behind each of those fronts. Maybe nothing. Maybe it was all an illusion, like the tricks Nadine herself used so successfully.

"Some day you're going to get tired of all this hanky-panky and find yourself alone, Kid, when it's too late," O'Flannery reminded her suddenly.

With her mind still on her work, Nadine looked over at him in surprise. "This hanky-panky has done pretty well for me . . . and you too, up to now. When did you go moral on me?"

"I was referring to your bedtime hanky-panky."

Embarrassed, and bad-tempered because she was embarrassed, Nadine bit off "Forget it!" which sounded to her sharp and cutting enough to discourage any man. She wished she had answered him more mildly, soothingly. Well, it was too late now!

"They really pull in the sidewalks here at midnight, don't they?" she remarked shortly after, hoping to get him onto another subject and in a better humor.

"Hardly. Most of the Spa bunch is either swilling it down in the Gold Room or sexing it up at the Hot Springs. They just don't do it out here in the street." He looked out, frowning. "If you can call this a street. You're right about one thing. There's not a light anywhere. Those little street lights, but they just make the dark around them—"

"—darker," she put in with what was meant to be a laugh, but there was an hysterical tinge to it. Still, with a furtive side-glance at him, she hoped they were friends again.

He stopped the car at a tiny bridge that forded the dusty, gravel-strewn creek bed. Beyond was the mountainside, heavy with shadows where the dry brush drained off the slanting moonlight. He reached across her body and opened the door.

"Out, Princess. This buggy won't climb that trail. The rest is up to you."

It was no comfort to know she had nobody to thank but herself that she must climb the trail to her temple alone and in a tight, floor-length satin skirt. She started to get out, stopped a few seconds as he added flatly but—she thought—with a tiny shred of hope, "Unless you've changed your mind. That Blue-Green Room at the Spa where the pool is . . . pretty sweet against the skin this hour of the night."

That was true enough. She almost agreed. But she was already getting out of the car and in doing so, she stepped on her skirt, tearing the hem. The maddening little accident made her decision for her. She always accepted a dare and she always challenged a blackmailer. O'Flannery, knowing she feared walking up the mountain at this hour alone, was blackmailing her. She had to challenge him tonight or lose control of her own life.

"You're probably right. But you'll find someone in there, even at this hour. Have fun, Darling."

She knew she had tripped him up. He waited. Either he expected her to change her mind, or he was too angry to move. She turned, hearing her shoe grate unnervingly on the gravel. She waved to him, smiling.

He didn't return the wave. But she could see in the faint afterglow of the car lights that he didn't look angry either. He look puzzled, even sad. Depressing thought! She did not want him sad. Then he backed up, turned the car with screeching noises that would have awakened anyone at this end of the village, always assuming there were people behind those dark, blank facades.

Dark. But blank? "I must look into that some day," she thought and started across the bridge. She wished the clicking sound of her heels did not carry so far in the still night.

She decided to concentrate on her profession: How to bring out more than the showmanship angle for the Coven. She had seldom failed in putting on shows that dazzled the beholders, enticing members from every group: the Beautiful

People, hoping to make a deal with the powers of darkness, to retain what they had; the menopausal problem children—male and female—grasping at what had slipped past them; the young ones full of zodiac wonders they thought they had invented.

It would really be an accomplishment to persuade these followers that she had positive powers, powers which helped these sad, seeking human beings. She could scare them, and amaze them, titillate them . . . the ridiculous sex orgies that the members expected. But all these petty triumphs did not quite give her the satisfaction she had hoped for. She found she now wanted self-respect as well.

A late night breeze whirled through the underbrush and across her face, carrying with it the pleasantly bitter tang of the dry shrubs, and she snapped out of her uneasy dreams, the build up plans that usually filled her hours. She had climbed rapidly the last few minutes and when she turned and looked back down the winding path, she was surprised at how far she had come. The car had long since been parked in the lot back of the Spa and she could imagine O'Flannery taking a bottle and retiring to his room. Unless, of course, he chose to invade the pool and make a pass at one of the Super-Rich, physically well-endowed clients. She hoped he wouldn't.

"They don't understand him the way I do." He could hurt them by his indifference, his crazy attitude that he was somehow not part of the human race. Or worse, they could hurt him. That mattered a great deal more.

"A little more of this and I'll begin to think I

am jealous," she told herself with wry amusement. It was amusing because if there was one thing in an unsure world that she could be sure of, it was O'Flannery's loyalty to her. Their meeting during a cable car accident on the steep, Hyde Street line, had been one of those reversals of the usual heroic encounter that was bound either to make friends for life or a noisy lawsuit. It was the hundred pound Nadine who dragged all hundred and eighty pounds of the Irishman out from under the gripman's jammed brake. She claimed forever after that her Scorpio horoscope for the day had predicted a chance of a huge investment, and he was the biggest investment she ran into that day.

She had never since been able to pry herself loose from O'Flannery, who claimed that, having saved his life—or at the very least, his left leg—she inherited the leg and it was hers for its lifetime. Unavoidably, he reminded her, he went along with the inherited leg. She had not always regretted the inheritance.

The little valley looked silent and dead as a Necropolis in the moonlight, all but the cluster of lights in the Hot Springs at the far end of the valley, where she knew from experience that the varied oddities of sexual taste were catered to, with results worthy of Ovid's Roman pleasures. In fact, several enjoyments of the Ancients, now much practiced, were Nadine's suggestions. She made only one stipulation, that she herself did not participate.

Her open-sandaled evening shoe slipped on a flat piece of shale and she barely caught herself before slipping over the edge of the narrow path.

She could hardly have tumbled to her death at the bottom in the dry creek bed, but she would have been badly battered against the shrubs, twisted tree trunks and the debris of a dry summer. The effort to save herself cost her the painful wrenching of the muscles in her right forearm and she groaned with pain as she recovered her equilibrium. At the same time, standing quite still, she thought she heard a footstep on the path above her. The temple was only a couple of hundred yards overhead, and she found it even more upsetting that someone might be prowling around the building, ruining all her carefully worked up effects.

She pulled herself together, ignoring the pulled muscle, and the fragility of her shoes, and hurried on up to the little shelf of ground where an ambitious raw food health resort had once been planned and whose sole monument was the white-pillared Grecian Temple. The faint, bluish halo of light that outlined the pillars revealed no intruders in the outer portico, but she slipped up to the steps in the deep shadow of the mountainside, wondering what she would do if several troublemakers were here tearing up the place. She had a beretta hidden behind the makeup mirror in her dressing room if she could get to it. She had never fired it, and O'Flannery scoffed at the gun, claiming it fired off and misfired more than it fired. But it was a gun and it wasn't as heavy as some of the others she had examined. Actually, the beretta's value to her was more in its presence than its ability to fire straight.

She went quietly up the steps next to the portico wall and saw that the center doors were ajar.

someone really was inside. She slipped along close to the doors, opened one in a gingerly way and with a bone-rattling shock, found herself face to face with Marc Meridon, the exceedingly attractive young mystery man who owned a piece of the Spa and had, it was said, an investment in the Hot Springs as well.

"Good evening, Miss Janos. I hope I didn't startle you."

Looking at him and finding her anger softened by his charm, she thought the checkroom girl at the Cafe Madrigal was right. He really did have remarkably fine eyes, large, luminous and very dark. Curiously sad in spite of his delightful smile. He was a slight man of little more than middle height, not at all formidable. And scarcely over thirty. It had been absurd to go running all over Northern California doing research on his background. He simply recognized in Nadine a good investment and had helped her out in the hope of investing with her, no doubt.

She laughed. "I thought there were vandals in here. Thank heaven it is you." She let him close the door, reaching over her head to do so.

"Yes. I rather fancied there were some intruders up here. I saw moving lights about half an hour ago. I was returning from a long walk; so I came over to look 'round." His pleasant voice had just the hint of an accent which she claimed was London Theatre English, but which O'Flannery thought had a slight brogue of some kind. Edna Schallert, an old-maidish cultist, on the other hand, had beeen willing to bet he was French or Belgian and Irena Byaglu said he was Macedonian. The truth probably was somewhere in between all these exotic notions.

Belatedly, she worried over his last words. "What did you find, Mr. Meridon? Is everything all right?" She went past him, looking along the center aisle toward the altar with its inverted cross carved, as Nadine always carefully explained, from a stake used in the Middle Ages to destroy a suspected vampire. When she said this, Nadine had always shrugged and smiled, explaining, "whether the poor box of bones actually was a vampire, I cannot say. But in any case, the bones were nailed to the coffin by the wooden stake which is the original of that cross."

Marc Meridon watched her hurrying around the long, bare room with its full-length black-curtained windows, which served as her center for the cult's worship activities.

"Do you find anything wrong? Anything missing?"

"Not so far. I wonder . . ." She crossed the dais that served as an altar, and searched the back rooms briefly. Most of these were kept locked to prevent any of the Devil Worshippers from getting too many ideas. She knew the disaster to all her careful effects if their simple secrets were known. She tried the doors now and found two of them unlocked. Nothing seemed to be missing. One was a little dressing room containing her black and white costumes and a fold-up cot laid out and ready for her occupancy, with its clean, stiff white sheets. Nothing tinted, dyed, madly floral. She could not find the key and closed the door anxiously, running along the narrow, dark hall toward the black-shaded altar light.

"Mr. Meridon, someone has been in here. I always keep these rooms locked, and O'Flannery double checks after me."

Meridon came down the aisle and without glancing at the altar, stepped up on the dias and met her. He seemed puzzled by her complaint.

"I didn't notice. Are you sure? Shall we try the doors?"

She thought it a useless gesture but knew that it was always necessary to prove things to men. They never took a woman's word for anything. She backed up, demonstrated by turning the door knob and, surprisingly, found that this time the door was locked. Probably it had not been properly closed and the lock hadn't caught. Simple enough if you looked for a simple cause.

Marc Meridon smiled, asked if he might escort her down to her suite in the Spa and when she refused politely, he left her. She walked out to the portico and watched his slim figure gradually become a part of the darkness on the path below the temple.

If he had been up in San Francisco at the Cafe Madrigal a few hours ago, he must have used to good advantage the half hour that she and O'Flannery had been stopped by the accident. What was he really doing up here at the temple? Remembering those doors that had been open and now locked easily, she went back into the temple and directly to one of the rooms whose lock had given her trouble. With fingers surprisingly nervous, she looked for and located the correct key on her key ring. When she had opened the door, she looked around, going rapidly over the contents of the room but unable to find anything missing.

She finally decided that even if Meridon had spent time in the rooms, searching for heaven knew what?—he had found nothing. Maybe he told the truth. He had seen moving lights here and walked over from the Valley Peak Trail to challenge the intruders. Still, it was really none of his business. And if three or four tough kids were prowling through here, Marc Meridon would have been no match for them.

She looked out the window. The moon was overhead now, and cast short, abrupt shadows, nothing to alarm her. Nor were there sounds, except a cricket somewhere nearby. Still, she was beginning to wish she had not been so quick to get rid of O'Flannery and Meridon. There was an unpleasant sensation of company in the temple with her. Life of some sort that huddled in the dark, waiting for Nadine to go off guard.

"Come, now, you coward," she lashed herself, turning away from the window determined to face down any such ideas. She had to prove that she didn't need O'Flannery or anyone else, because of course, it was his absence that triggered these terrors.

She walked through the temple's back rooms, reaching for and snapping on the concealed electric light switches, then, having satisfied herself that hers was the only presence, snapped the lights off. Generally, at the time of Devil Worship Services, the rooms left unlocked were lighted by candles and their graceful electric imitations. Tiny globes whose lights seemed to flicker with just enough suggestion of "eerie winds from the netherworld" to induce shivers in the expectant Coven. The trouble was, such imaginative schemes backfired. Nadine had now managed to scare herself! She laughed at the ironic thought, but the sound seemed to ripple through the hall and bounce back like dozens of brittle sounds exploding from all directions.

In the main hall itself, the corners were dark but the nave, as it was sacrilegiously called, caught some of the glow from the concealed lighting around the pillars out in the portico. With her back to the altar, she stared down at the hall, seeing in her mind's eye, the congregation staring up at her hypnotized. Sometimes these hopeful, half-believing stares troubled her. She realized briefly how wasteful and wasted her talents were. But fortunately for her peace of mind, such self-doubts could be banished in short order.

She set her jaw and swung around, once again a hundred pounds of what one of her followers called "dynamic tension."

"I'll bed down on the cot, wake up with the sun shining, and laugh at all this. And I'll never let O'Flannery know."

No sound warned her. No intuition. She glanced up casually at the top of the inverted cross on the altar, smiled at the source of that blackened wood—the stake that had pierced the bones of some forgotten unfortunate in the Middle Ages—and then became aware of a light behind it, in mid-air. Or was it twin lights? She blinked. Her imagination was really working overtime. From somewhere, probably the all-night portico lights, a combination of circumstances had begun to form certain features in mid-air. Hardly human, those eyes deep burning as they followed her sudden, shocked move. But they were eyes, and not her trick conjuring.

She rocked on her heels, took hasty steps backward, felt herself falling off the dais, and this time even her taut muscles did not save her.

THREE

"Good Lord!" thought Nadine, opening her eyes and wincing at the daylight that sifted in through the hot-pink drapes. "I've been seduced into that damned Hot Springs."

It had always been a sore point between her and O'Flannery. He called her "phony." She encouraged the Coven members to give in to their so-called baser instincts, "do what came natural" and find much of their erotic pleasure at the Springs. But Nadine herself had never even sampled the pleasures of the Hot Springs. And here she was, ensconced in style in one of those sybaritic rooms reserved for special, and wealthy clients of Lucifer Cove.

Someone stirred behind her and she asked, with a sudden vivid memory of last night's accident. "Could anything be done for those kids who crashed into us?"

A male voice with a Northern, probably German accent, spoke behind her. "But that is not how you took that so-unpleasant blow on the back of the head, Miss Janos. You were up at your temple and apparently you tripped and fell backward. You do not remember?"

"Oh, that! I fell off the dais. Clumsy." She shifted her position on the unexpectedly glamorous pink satin pillow, and groaned. There was a painful spot at the back of her head, though she did not seem to be bandaged anywhere. She frowned. The male voice behind her was annoying, the way it kept probing for what had happened up there at the temple.

"A curious thing for you to do, Miss Janos. You are not clumsy. We here in the village have often remarked upon the grace and dignity with which you move."

She was not entirely gratified. She thought he was fishing for some description of that absurb fantasy which made her lose her balance. In the warm, dusty daylight she guessed without hesitation that those weird eyes staring at her in midair had been nothing but a ridiculous combination of lights and shadows. Even the memory of those eyes, unreal as they were, made her shudder. She pretended, however, that the shudder was due to some lingering remnant of her headache.

"Does it hurt?"

She raised her head, said "no" before she thought and then caught a faint narrowing of the eyes of the doctor as he appeared within her range. She had seen Dr. Erich Haupt around Lucifer Cove upon occasion and thought him a curious, tall thin fellow with noticeably pallid flesh, keen dark eyes and a mouth whose upper lip was harshly repressive and lower lip a violent, voluptuous opposite. He had none of the attractions so obvious in other men at the Cove, men like O'Flannery and Marc Meridon, but she was intensely aware of this man around her now. He seemed to be a person of unsuspected power, perhaps less physical than mental. While she was not immune to the Irishman or Meridon, this Dr. Haupt was a challenge in her own field of mental powers. She returned his stare with all the effort she could muster.

He had taken her wrist in his thin, hard-boned fingers, but she could judge the precise second when his interest shifted from her pulse to her face, her real *self*. She projected all her potent appeal through her remarkable, smoky blue eyes.

"So?" he began in his slightly Germanic way. "You are the little lady in league with the devil."

She timed her smoky gaze carefully, lowered it just at the right second, while he was still held by it, and murmured, "You probably find my work ridiculous." And she added, in an attitude of very feminine defense, "But it's no worse than astrology. I mean—well, we do produce results."

"Results? But yes. I am full of curiosity."

"People get their wishes. That sort of thing."

He returned her wrist to her. "Yes. That is good. You were lucky, Miss Janos. You seem to have gotten no more than a bump on the head. It might have been serious. Perhaps your friend, the devil, was at your side."

"What!" Suspicious, she stared at him. He couldn't possibly know what had happened up there to cause this fall. Or could he?

He shrugged. "You have had luck. Some would say—'Thanks be to God.' But you, you may say: 'Thanks be to the Devil'."

She exhaled, grinning in a way that made her look very young. "That! Yes, I suppose I can say that. I've got to admit, though, that from long habit I do bring up God every once in a while." She balled her hand into a fist, plumped up the silly, sexy satin pillow, and settled back in a sitting position. Her head gave a little twinge, but that was to be expected and it meant nothing. Dr. Haupt was right. She really could have been worse off. Far worse. She said comfortably, "You're right. I do appreciate getting off easy."

"It may be that you should offer up thanks to those little demons you consort with in your temple," he reminded her with a toothy smile. There was something familiar about him, either his looks or his manner. Not in his smile, but when he talked, when he gesticulated almost mechanically. She felt she had seen him somewhere before but couldn't place him. The small problem needled her. However, his remark was clearly meant as a joke and she took him up on it.

"I may do just that. By the way, why don't you come up and see our show some night?"

"We have our own show here, Miss Janos. It is a disappointment that we do not see you at the Hot Springs now and then."

Very likely! She thought: "I've got better things to do with my time than carry on sodomy, or the Lesbian bit, or the rest of it here in this dark, sensuous, perfumed netherworld." But she did not say this aloud. It would be difficult to explain why some of the "social activities" of the Hot Springs had been suggested by Nadine herself.

"I'm sorry. I've been frantically busy. I'm afraid I simply never have time for those cute games you play here at the Springs. Maybe later on, when I have more time. How am I?"

Dr. Haupt wrote something on her chart, called in a tall statuesquely beautiful nurse with showgirl proportions and informed Nadine that she seemed unhurt, "except for the contusions, and a nasty bump on the sub-cranial..."

"In other words, I am well enough to leave."

"But we prefer that you stay the night. Just to be certain of no after effects. You understand." He and the nurse exchanged glances of subtle amusement. It was quick, unobtrusive, but Nadine did not miss it. She began to be uneasy.

"Impossible. I have work to do tonight."

"I'm afraid I must insist," he contradicted suavely.

This threatened to be serious. Was it possible these far-out cornballs with their "hospital" facilities carefully set up on the second floor of the main Hot Springs building, expected to convert Nadine Janos to those famous *Nights?* Maybe this, with a few properly administered drugs, explained that final corruption of so many Lucifer Cove clients. She had wondered about that... The curious way the least sensual people, whose one passion was money, or power, began to disport themselves sexually at the Hot Springs. Ultimately the end was self-destruction. Suicide —which generally managed to preclude the shock of heart failure from over-exertion, or even the more lingering unpleasantness of less sociably acceptable diseases.

Nadine wanted no part of it. On the other hand, she knew she was no match for the bosomy nurse, much less her tall, sinister boss, Dr. Haupt. Though Nadine could almost admire his technique because it certainly worked. She settled back again after the tense moment or two when she realized her possible danger. With some slight effort she managed to pretend an innocence of their intentions. It was not difficult to further pretend her sole interest was in her work.

"Well, in that case changes have to be made. That lazy Irishman! I'll need him for the temple business tonight. I'll bet he's somewhere sleeping one off. Damn it! Never here when I need him. If I could just get my hands on him, I wouldn't be so worried about tonight."

"But Dear Miss Janos, nothing is easier. Why have you not said you wished to see this Mr. Flannery? You do not remember how you came here in the night? It was by the arms of this Flannery?"

"O'Flannery," she corrected him automatically, beginning to understand. "So that's who found me up there! Good Lord! He must have carried me down that trail."

He laughed. "It is true. You do call upon what you Americans call the Good Guys, and yet you are priestess to the Bad Guys."

"It depends on your point of view. Can you send for O'Flannery?"

He inclined his head slightly. She almost imagined he would click his heels. He refrained, however. As he left the room, his tall figure in its stiff, starched white seemed to return to her original estimate of him as a mere trickster who used the Hot Springs as she used the temple, to promote himself in his chosen business. Perhaps those wise looks that passed between him and his nurse had not meant what she suspected at all. Funny, the ideas, suspicions that haunted her. She couldn't seem to escape them. She saw evil, even horror, in everything that approached her.

All but O'Flannery. She had treated him shabbily and yet he must have known she would need him. He had come at some mysterious summons from her subconscious. Bless him!

Devil Bless him! Oh well . . . She reached around for the makeup in her handbag but found neither. O'Flannery had goofed on that. She hurriedly smoothed her hair, wondering if she would need to have her hair tinted within the next few days. There might be a small problem about the bump on her head, but her weekly "dye job" was absolutely necessary. Her naturally blonde hair took away all the mystery, all the power which experience had taught that her face possessed.

Several people, mostly nurses, came by her open door and peeked in at her. Whether she interested them as a potential client or as the High Priestess of the Devil's Coven, she could not tell. In spite of her dislike of the setup here, she hoped she did not look too bad. Even her enemies must be disarmed if she was to keep her prestigious position among the impressionable.

She heard the Irishman before he arrived. His teasing voice was regaling someone—it had to be a female, and pretty!—with his usual charm. She stiffened, expecting the worst, and it came. The girl with O'Flannery was leggy, tallish, with deep auburn hair which she wore to her shoulders in an old-fashioned curly mass, wind-blown, a loose tendril occasionally beating against her hollowed, high-boned cheeks. A model on the loose, obviously. She was wearing a pink satin smock, the uniform of the young women at Lucifer Cove who helped out in the hospital at the

Hot Springs. As Nadine understood it, they contributed their personal charms, bodily and mentally, to the entertainment of the Hot Springs crowd, thus entitling themselves to remain and share in the sybaritic luxury of Lucifer Cove without that important requisite, money.

The girl made an enchanting little moué with her pale pink lips as they entered Nadine's room. She was clearly explaining that she was not mad about the Hot Springs but that she had been at loose ends and someone suggested the Cove to give her time to recover her equilibrium. Whatever that entailed, Nadine thought.

O'Flannery was horribly casual in greeting Nadine, just when it was important that he be warm, show his concern for her, and with that revolting redhaired beauty getting primed, obviously ready for the romantic fallout.

"Well, Princess, how's the hangover this everlovin' mornin'?" He kissed her breezily on the forehead. She smiled, refrained with difficulty from kissing the rugged, not quite shaved line of his cheek. She was unable to bear the thought of that redhead seeing that she cared so much, that she was vulnerable. That was how they got their hooks in and twisted, these beauties, these women who made it the easy way.

Nadine said instead, "Wrong as usual, Love. That was no drunken fall. As a matter of fact, I was sober as a priest. Or a priestess." Then she wished she hadn't argued the point. It was stupid to remind him of the real cause of her fall. Better to let him and particularly his companion think it was the drinks at the Madrigal that belatedly caused Nadine to tumble off the dais. If anyone guessed the truth, she would be written off as kookier than her followers!

He had leaned over to kiss her, and straightened during her protest, then stopped all movement briefly, studying her face. "Only putting you on. Araby here wanted to meet you. So I brought her along."

Araby! Shades of the 'Twenties! "How nice to meet you, Miss—Is it Araby as in *Shiek of?*" She asked, trying not to sound too catty.

"No," the girl corrected her in a flip, easy voice. "Araby as in *Perfumes of.*"

Nadine and O'Flannery laughed and the redhaired girl, not redhaired for nothing, went on "I've always thought your own name was fascinating, Miss Janos. Did you choose it because of the Roman god? I mean . . . the two-faced analogy?"

Nadine blinked rapidly. Her fingers curled around the hem of the satin sheet and O'Flannery covered them with his own hand until they were still again.

"I had no choice in the matter of names. It was my father's. If he had another face to show the world and me, I certainly wish he'd use it."

This time the laughter was general and the redhaired girl looked suddenly warm, winning. "I always get uptight about my name. You see, it's Arabella, and I model. Avedon and the new top boys aren't looking for a lacy shawl named Arabella. Glad to've met you, Miss Janos. Everybody hopes to see you around the Hot Springs one of these nights."

"Too busy at the moment. Maybe later. How about dropping in on the services at the temple one of these nights. Come along any time. Who knows? You may have a wish granted you?"

The redhead grinned in the doorway before disappearing. "I'd have to work up a wish first. Maybe I will. 'Bye, Ducks."

"Who is Ducks?" Nadine wanted to know when they were alone.

O'Flannery ignored this. He sat down on the edge of the bed and playfully slapped the sheet over her thighs.

"Now, what's it all about? I hope you know what you're in for in this place. A lot of warm persuasion about the thrills of group-love."

She sat up, ignoring the little, needling headache. There was work to do. "Never mind that. How do I get out of here? That's the big question. Dr. Haupt has the place full of muscular horrors, female gender, who would probably break me in two with a karate chop if I get past the door. I may be flattering myself, but I think he figures if he got me capering with his oversexed customers, it would somehow add to his take. Assure them he had the devil on his side, you might say."

"I don't doubt it." He was studying her soberly, with care. "What does he say about you? You seem your salty self, but that fall knocked you out a long time. That and the gook they gave you."

She didn't doubt it. "Why on earth did you bring me here? You know what the damned place is like."

"That's gratitude! What else was I supposed to do? I carried you down that trail. I could've driven you to Carmel or Monterey, but for all I

41

knew, you could have been dead by that time. What happened up there, anyway? It isn't like you to be so clumsy."

She treated the matter offhandedly, blaming her fall on the fact that the lights were out and she had misjudged her steps, but she was fairly certain she hadn't fooled him. He was rarely fooled about her for very long. He looked at her in silence, briefly, then got up and went across the room to the door which the model, Araby, had left ajar. But no one was out there, and after glancing in each direction, he turned back to Nadine, making plans.

"I take it you don't want to just walk out with me and thumb your nose at this gang."

"I wouldn't mind, but if he did stop us, claiming I was too sick or something, it would be harder to sneak by him later."

He agreed. Knowing O'Flannery, she was sure his head had been full of schemes, even while he suggested a simple, uncomplicated walkout. "Sure you're all right, though? No tricks now, Princess."

"I've got to be all right," she reminded him, surprised that he should have forgotten. "The Coven is meeting tonight."

"That's not what I meant. And I hadn't forgotten. No headaches? No spots before the eyes? No Gray Sickness?" He was prodding her over the head and neck and except for the original bump whose swelling made her wince, she had recovered all her nervous energy.

She disentangled herself from the slippery satin sheets and got up, triumphantly waving aside his helping hand. She swayed for a few seconds, recovered and demanded to know what they were to do. His first suggestion didn't go down at all well.

"I'll get the redhead. We can use her."

"Not that Araby creature!" she cried in a panic as he left. "What makes you think you can trust her? She's bound to be in this with her employer."

"She's only a volunteer, and Haupt is not strictly speaking, her employer." He was already striding out in the hall. She gave up, hoping for the best.

While she rustled around, looking first under the bed, then reaching for the closet door where she devoutly hoped to find her street clothes, she heard Dr. Haupt's remembered accents in the hall. She made a violent effort, landed on the bed and was just pulling down the skimpy skirt of the so-called Hospital Gown when Dr. Haupt reached the door and pushed it open.

"You might knock," she informed him. "That is, if you approve of the exercise, Doctor!"

His narrow eyes glittered in a way she found both unpleasant and challenging. The odd sense of familiarity returned. She couldn't recall any circumstances in which they might have met socially; yet there it was, a tingling sense of danger. It tantalized her chiefly because she couldn't place him.

"My dear Miss Janos, when one has—ah—charms such as yours, there can be no crime greater than to conceal them."

If she hadn't been so keyed up, she would have laughed at this corny line. It was not so much that she doubted her own assets. It was merely

43

that she doubted their effect upon a man who witnessed, and doubtless participated in what Lucifer Cove called a Sex Factory. He did not miss her scowl, which made him slightly suspicious. He started into the room.

"How are you feeling, Miss Janos? You have a trifle—only a trifle of pallor, but I think I must prescribe for you a sedative. Something that will prevent these tossings and turnings. All this movement does not assist your recovery.

A little breathless with nerves, and trying to hide it, Nadine protested too quickly, "No, no, really, I can't think of anything I need less. I'm perfectly calm. In fact, I was getting ready to take a nap when you spoke."

Dr. Haupt was much closer, his manner and his voice horrifyingly sweet. "Now then, you are lying to ease our concern over you. You really must not do this. It is our business to make you well." He reached toward her, and it took all her resolution to keep from cringing away from those hard, bony fingers. Belatedly, she discovered he was ringing for the nurse.

"Please," she tried again. "I wish you wouldn't. I don't need it. I'm really rather sleepy."

"You are really rather a charming liar, Miss Janos. I'll wager at this moment you are wishing you might rush off to your mountain peak and summon up demons for the ignorant peasantry. No, no. Here, it is my job to cure my patients." He rang again, then dropped the cord. It hit the bed with a metallic noise that made her jump and caused him to nod as if this were proof of his diagnosis.

When she heard steps again in the hall, she

hoped against hope that it might be O'Flannery, but she knew it wasn't. His walk was much louder, a loping walk. Not quiet and direct and inevitable like the sounds she heard now.

FOUR

She was almost afraid to look at Dr. Haupt but as the footsteps clearly were audible to them both, she could not resist sneaking a look to judge his reaction. She thought the flat, Nordic planes of his face looked oddly tense. Perhaps he was afraid it was the big Irishman and pictured endless difficulties ahead, including O'Flannery's slightly tipsy violence.

She was both relieved and surprised to see Marc Meridon passing by the open door. Although his generally youthful look and stripling slenderness did not suggest much of a defense against the hard-boned doctor, he was a welcome sight to Nadine. She called to him. When he turned, she crooked her finger in a beckoning gesture. He smiled, stepped inside the room and looked at Dr. Haupt.

"Am I permitted? How is the patient?"

"Fine. Ready to sign out," Nadine said quickly before the doctor could put a twist in her escape. She glanced at him, trying to build up her mental agility to argue against his negative report on her. But he was eyeing Meridon curiously, not denying her words. She took the chance. "Don't you agree, Doctor?"

He hesitated. This unsure moment she sensed

in Erich Haupt was puzzling and distinctly against his previous attitude.

She was grateful when Marc Meridon's quiet voice seemed to settle the matter. "I am going over to the Spa. Miss Janos has a comfortable suite there. From what Mr. O'Flannery tells me about her injury, she is quite well enough to leave here. What do you think, Doctor?"

Dr. Haupt shrugged, in none too good a mood. "Then I am to understand the Irish gentleman is still here wandering through the halls? I sincerely hope he does not disturb my other patients. He does give the impression of the bull in the china shop." He made a sudden, impatient movement as if, Nadine thought, he wanted to take his anger out on O'Flannery. "I must go and see that he makes no trouble."

She had no fear for the Irishman. When Erich Haupt had left her room, she turned to Meridon with an amusement that held some anxiety, "Thank you, more than I can say. He looks to me like a man who isn't safe to cross. I hope I haven't caused trouble over this."

He was looking rather thoughtfully after the doctor and she suspected he might be realizing the truth of her warning, but when he answered her, he seemed to be on the verge of a smile.

"I doubt it. But I appreciate your concern. I promised your friend O'Flannery not to detain you very long; so I'll leave you to dress." At her nervous look toward the door, he added reassuringly, "There should be no further problems." In his unobtrusive way he almost convinced her.

When he had gone and Nadine was getting into last night's highly inappropriate black and white evening gown she found hanging in the closet, it came to her suddenly why Marc Meridon was able to beard the sinister Dr. Haupt in his lair. Undoubtedly, some of Meridon's money was invested in the Hot Springs. She wished more than ever that she had learned something about him yesterday in San Francisco. Like many of the Big Money men, he was clearly secretive about his investments, and his friends, or partners, knew better than to betray him.

She wondered how she could wangle some information about him from his acquaintances at the Cove. Christine Deeth must know. The beautiful Mrs. Deeth had come to the Cove less than six months ago, fresh from a messy divorce. But she was Marc Meridon's mistress now, and the relationship gave every sign of being as permanent as anything else at the Cove. There were moments when Nadine envied Christie Deeth. She was not blind to Meridon's attractions, physical as well as financial.

"Too bad," Nadine sighed to herself. "For me, it would never work, even if Meridon did go for me—and he certainly doesn't!" The stupid, obvious hospital gown had done nothing for her, in Meridon's eyes. On the other hand, Nadine knew herself well enough to be certain she could only pursue her work while she was her own boss. Any relationship with men like Marc Meridon, men of money and influence, would be cancelled out the first time she refused to take orders. Dr. Erich Haupt, on the other hand, repulsive as his business was, might fit in much better as a business associate, possibly because she despised him.

The redhaired model, Araby, showed up with

her arm cosily in O'Flannery's, a sight not calculated to calm Nadine's high state of nerves, but she managed to subdue her jealousy when Marc Meridon arrived immediately after. Araby was in the process of offering to loan Nadine her lipstick but Meridon obligingly remarked,

"You do not need it, Miss Janos. You are more effective without it."

Whatever that meant!

When they left the hospital wing, Nadine left it to the others to find the little party's way out of the labyrinth. And it was a labyrinth, with so many confusing halls, marble, mosaic, parquetry-paved, all tantalizing in their mystery and petty grandeur, that she was almost tempted to stay and explore them.

"What a place for my Coven to meet!" she remarked to Meridon, having chosen his arm and his company to spite O'Flannery who strode ahead of them with Araby, but kept looking back to see what they were up to.

"Really? How so?"

"Because it's so—so sybaritic," she explained. "People always expect to find devils in rich, fancy settings. It's the Christian myth. The Good Guys live in poverty. The Bad Guys live it up. I must say, I've always been with the Bad Guys at heart."

"To reign is worth ambition,
  though in Hell."

She looked at him, startled. "Exactly my sentiments. You do understand!" She saw his eyes then, the sombre darkness that women at the Cove admired so much. She had thought he was only amusing her with the quotation from Paradise Lost, but she saw now that Milton did not really amuse him.

"I know!" she cried quickly, seeing that O'Flannery was looking back at them again. "But my favorite part comes later. That wonderful line of Satan's . . ." She declaimed dramatically, "'Better to reign in hell than serve in heaven.' That's my philosophy."

"'Better to reign in hell than serve in heaven,'" Meridon repeated, adding, "How well the old Puritan knew life and death, heaven and hell! One would think he had been there, observed—" He laughed shortly. "Poetic truth, you see. I am an admirer of poets. I have known a few."

"I can imagine. They always need money." Then she was intrigued by the ease with which he and the pair in front of them found their way to the heated pools outside, an area with which Nadine was more familiar, having bathed there several times. She discovered, watching Meridon and Araby carefully, that they were guided by the scarlet line painted along the baseboard of the stark white wall. There were other lines leading off from the Admissions Desk through other halls, blue in one direction, green, deep gold and a sinister black in other directions. Nadine had never before gotten, or wanted to get, any further into the labyrinth. But there was no doubt it had intriguing possibilities for exploration. The trouble was, her interest remained academic, not physical.

She breathed deeply of the warm, sultry air in the main street of the village, then began to cough as she inhaled sulphur fumes from the therapeutic baths.

"This is as far as I go for now," Araby announced, slapping O'Flannery on the arm in a comradely way that surprised the watchful Nadine. "Got to get back and scrub a few floors, empty a few bedpans."

Nadine called her thanks after the girl who waved without looking around. Nadine expected Marc Meridon to leave too, but as they were joined by O'Flannery, Meridon remarked suddenly, in a troubled way, "You coughed, a minute ago, Miss Janos. But would you say this is an unhealthy place to live?"

"Unhealthy! Certainly not." What was he driving at? Morally, Lucifer Cove was no Religious Retreat, but otherwise, it had proved remarkably healthy. She could seldom recall seeing anyone with the usual ailments: viruses, or respiratory or rhuematic diseases. And those who drove themselves to drug addiction or delirium tremens soon disappeared into Dr. Haupt's clinic.

"You figure on setting up a cure for the Common Cold?" O'Flannery asked, eyeing Meridon curiously.

"Not that, no. But a friend of mine, Mrs. Deeth, has a ten-year-old son who is just recovering from Spinal Meningitis. I have suggested to her that the waters here would be beneficial, and the sunlight. The mountainside paths to strengthen the boy's left leg—the muscles were weakened by the disease. What do you think?"

Nadine and O'Flannery exchanged puzzled glances. Nadine, in particular, began to suspect she might have found the reason why Meridon had gone to such great lengths to get her out of Dr. Haupt's delightful House of Debauchery. He wanted a favor in return. She did not mind, nor was she disillusioned. She was only suspicious when people went out of their way to help one another with no expectation of payment. Before O'Flannery could throw a wrench in the idea, Nadine spoke up, hoping to give the Irishman his cue.

"Personally—and I am no authority on it—I would say the boy might be helped. In the Santa Cruz Mountains to the North they have any number of spas and camps and health resorts. The climate here doesn't seem to have harmed anyone. You never see anyone sick."

"Only suicides," O'Flannery put in, with a wry grin.

Nadine could not have said why she was made uneasy by the glance that Marc Meridon gave to the Irishman at this remark. Meridon's look was perfectly expressionless. Nevertheless, she said brusquely, "Shut up!" and saw that Marc Meridon had amusedly noted the sharp intimacy between them. He studied the enveloping mountain peaks everywhere around them and she followed his attention. He frowned. He seemed a kindly man, generous and helpful and devastatingly attractive; yet some intuition told her he could be a ruthless competitor in his own business, whatever that was. Perhaps almost as ruthless as the sinister Dr. Haupt. But so much more charming about it!

What kind of lover was he? She wished she could ask Christie Deeth, but that woman was so damned superior, as these jet-setting super-rich could be if they had never earned a dishonest dollar with their bare hands or busy brains. O'Flannery had once accused Nadine of being a snob. At her indignant denial, he pointed out that she always had contempt for people who hadn't made their own way in the world. Nadine's answer still seemed to make sense to her, though it had provoked a shake of the head and a spurt of laughter from the Irishman: "It isn't that I *think* I'm better than they are. I *know* I am. I must be! They couldn't do what I've done and succeed." It bewildered her when people couldn't see this naked fact.

And then, along came people like Christie Deeth who actually looked down on all Nadine's hard-won accomplishments. Fortunately, her boyfriend, Mr. Meridon, was not one of them. He said now, gratefully, "I would appreciate your persuading Mrs. Deeth that this is a healthy climate. Her husband and his new bride are taking a honeymoon cruise to the Orient, and since the boy wants to see his mother, and Christine is, of course, very anxious to be with him, she wants to go to San Francisco. But I think both Christine and Toby would be much better off here. It would be a vacation for the child, with warm pools to swim in, and the sun, and the paths for small, local hikes and exploring. The sort of holiday that children love."

"It sounds perfect to me. Don't you think so, Irish?" She glanced up at him with a warning frown he couldn't misread, but he did, saying innocently.

"Maybe it's Mrs. Deeth who wants a holiday."

Beside her, Nadine felt Marc Meridon stiffen

and take a sharp breath. She said in a loud, hurried voice, "That is ridiculous!" and added the rapidly shaded truth, "Only last week she told me this was perennial holiday, that she couldn't imagine her life anywhere else."

What Christie Deeth had actually said was in the nature of a remark to the pretty receptionist at the Spa, and overheard by Nadine: "I can't imagine ever having loved before. I've stopped asking myself whether it is a good love or a bad love. And with it all, he actually needs me, as I need him."

Perhaps Christie was talking about taking a vacation to San Francisco just to torment Meridon, to keep him "needing her." It was the sort of gesture Nadine could appreciate. "Still," she told herself honestly, "I shouldn't judge all women by my own conduct." She was surprised when Meridon stopped on the sidewalk in front of a bow-window toy shop and stared at Nadine, with a kind of desperate hope in his eyes that both touched and baffled her.

"Is this the truth, Miss Janos?"

She was quite ready to oblige him. It cost nothing, and besides, she suspected more and more that his good will could prove important to her and O'Flannery. She frowned at the Irishman who backed off with raised eyebrows. Then she lowered her voice, happy to repeat with perfect truth, "I can't imagine ever having loved before."

"What! Are you saying that you yourself . . . Or Christine?"

She assured him in haste, "That's precisely what Mrs. Deeth said. And then something about needing you and vice versa." She didn't know what to expect when he reached for her, and when Meridon hugged her like a boy passionately assured of his first love, she found herself blushing, partly at the pleasure she had so easily provided.

In the end, they parted at the entrance to the Spa, with her assurance that she would do her best to persuade Christie Deeth that Lucifer Cove would be an ideal summer resort for her crippled, ten-year old son. She left a note with Caro Teague, the girl at the desk, asking her to see that it was delivered to Mrs. Deeth at the earliest opportunity.

O'Flannery, who had heard more than she intended he should, disapproved of the whole business, just as she expected. They went in to the Spa's dining room, Nadine complaining about the erotic atmosphere of the restaurant whose darkness at noon, and peculiarly cozy banquettes were either an invitation to an immediate seduction, or a disaster area for diners with steak knives. Whenever Nadine saw that O'Flannery was about to get a word in—and it would be an unpleasant word—she went to work on another facet of her dining room criticism. But nothing prevented the steamroller.

"Keep out of it, Princess! I mean—*keep out!*"

"Don't tell me what to do. Besides, I'll only be helping two people in love. Maybe three, counting the child." The back of her head began to ache but she knew her excitement had triggered it.

The waiter was hovering, and O'Flannery stopped abruptly, rather to Nadine's surprise. She started to put up an argument and got an elbow in the ribs. This time, though belatedly, she shut up. O'Flannery had excellent reasons for such lapses from his normal indifference to the world and its problems.

A middle-aged, tense-looking woman across from them made a little signal of recognition to Nadine who had a sinking feeling at sight of her. She groaned, murmuring so low O'Flannery had to lean nearer to understand, "Oh, God! Edna Schallert looks suicidal again."

"Like the Byaglu."

She shivered. "Don't remind me!" Irena Byaglu, a client of the Cove and one of Nadine's own Coven, had begun the same way, with the same inexplicable depression, and Irena Byaglu had hanged herself in the Spa suite next to the one occupied by Mrs. Christine Deeth. Nadine didn't want a repetition of that ugly business.

"She's coming over," O'Flannery muttered unnecessarily.

Nadine girded her loins for the expected consolation performance. What the devil was the woman's birth date? Astrological consolation was a marvelous way out, with promises whose fulfillment would come at a future date, sufficiently distant.

Edna Schallert had never been a really attractive woman. Lacking beauty as a child she had neither the ambition nor the instinct to make something out of her personality. Or possibly she hadn't a personality with which to work. This was O'Flannery's theory, but then he had never known the anguish of being a small unattractive girl. Miss Schallert, at her present age of forty-eight, had one asset, the money left her by her parents. It had bought her the gigolo,

Gene Standish, who died here at the Cove and whose love with a price on it was not worth ten minutes of poor Edna's suffering. Nadine wished she could convince the woman of it. So far, no luck.

"Hello, Edna. Are you keeping busy?"

The woman was looking even thinner than usual, and so tense that the always high-keyed Nadine recognized the dangerous symptoms.

"I'm never busy. Never any more, Nadine. You know that. But I did want to consult you. Officially, that is. Are you free some time soon, before the Coven ceremonies tonight. I thought maybe we could offer up—you know—"

"Prayers to Our Lord Satan," said Nadine quickly.

"Yes. And maybe gifts would help." Her pale nervous eyes were hard to avoid, especially with O'Flannery standing there, taking it all in, waiting for the woman to go so he could resume his seat without too much impoliteness. He was sure to end by blaming Nadine and the plain fact was, she had nothing to do with Edna Schallert's dead boyfriend. They already had some kind of relationship going when Nadine first arrived at Lucifer Cove, so apparently the woman had found a bit of devilish help elsewhere to produce this sexual miracle in her starved life. As for donating money to the Service of My Lord Satan, as Nadine put it, that was strictly up to the worshippers. It so happened that Nadine's prayers—and sometimes the answers—were much stronger when the gifts and bequests were greater. The bequest from Irena Byaglu had been breathtaking, although it was not money that Nadine really, inside her heart, cared to think about. She had not believed what she so flippantly explained to O'Flannery, "Maybe the Devil is helping me through Irena. Obliging of him, I'm sure!"

"I'm very busy during the afternoon," Nadine began doubtfully, recalling the physical preparations, and even more important, the mental preparations necessary before a Coven meeting. "Must it be today?"

"Yes. Oh yes, Nadine. I need help so desperately. It's several things. The mirrors, for one thing. And animals look at me oddly. At least, one does. I had trouble before Gene's death, you remember. And now, it's all back again. I get the most awful feeling I'm being watched."

"Watched?" O'Flannery cut in, suddenly interested at this, the first actual symptom of her physical danger.

"Watched!" Edna Schallert repeated. And she went on, with a ghastly little gurgle of a laugh, "Watched, among other things, a feline. And even by my own furniture! You know how suggestive mirrors are."

This really opened O'Flannery's sleepy eyes. It took a considerable shaking up to do so. As for Nadine, she went through, in seconds, all the sensations of having lived this scene before, with grim and frightful results. Perhaps because she carried in her conscience a small, needling guilt over having failed Irena Byaglu months ago, she said abruptly, with anger, "Don't talk like that! Miss Byaglu was out of her mind. You've let something she said stick with you all this time. This sort of imaginary borrowing can be deadly. You have your own Thing, your own world. Don't borrow from a dead woman."

Edna Schallert looked so surprised she almost shed those aging wrinkles that formed a gridiron across her forehead. "Me?" But Nadine, I didn't even know that Miss Byaglu had these same awful-hallucinations."

O'Flannery motioned the woman to his seat. Her legs were unsteady but she backed off, with a quick, nervous refusal.

"I'd rather not, here in public. I mean, if I start telling you, somebody might hear."

Nadine looked around. The woman's panic was contagious. But aside from the sleek, serpentlike Ricardo Shahnaz, "dance instructor" at the Hot Springs, who was watching this end of the room with an oily grin, nobody looked very interested. In spite of Nadine's really startling success since her arrival in the valley, she had gradually come to feel that the trouble with Lucifer Cove was its close relationships. The whole valley behaved like a family enterprise. Everybody knew everybody else's affairs and privacy was difficult, if not impossible to achieve. Secrets were, in part, Nadine's stock in trade, but like the practical joker who can't take a joke, she loathed the possibility of anyone spying out those secrets she guarded for her clients. Her own secrets, she fancied, were miniscule, if they existed at all.

"All right, Miss Schallert. I'll make time for you. Say—later in the day. You might come in before the Coven meets. That won't be until after nine; so I can see you around seven or so. I do have to rest before the Services."

Edna Schallert understood this, or seemed to. She nodded with that eager intensity which made all her actions annoying in the extreme to the susceptible Nadine. The woman moved her thin, blue-veined hands jerkily up and down as she assured Nadine, "Of course you do. It must be a frightful strain, summoning up—*him*—from the depths, as it were."

Nadine tried to hush her, but Edna Schallert finished loudly with glassy-eyed triumph, "So I won't take up much of your precious time. But if I explain, and maybe you walk over to my chalet, it's not half a mile from your temple, you might exorcize whatever it is that's hounding me."

"Yes, yes. I'll see you. Between us, we'll do whatever we can, Miss Schallert. Take it easy until then." She hoped that would send the voluble, maddingly nervous woman on her way. People were looking their way now, the headwaiter, for example, an attractive Latin of uncertain age and impeccable manners. Nadine had nothing against the man and was not immune to his faintly aloof charm, but she suspected that he reported to Marc Meridon and the other Spa owners—whoever they were—any confidential matters he overheard here. The Spa's dining room was a more persistent meeting place than the blue-green pool or the mirrored cocktail room, and since both drinks and freely obtained drugs oiled the tongues of the Cove clients, a man judiciously stationed in the dining room could pick up enough blackmail material in a week to set him up for life.

Edna Schallert looked anxiously over her shoulder, caught the bland smile of the headwaiter, and leaned over Nadine to inform her hoarsely, "That man has a look of pure wickedness. I wouldn't be surprised if you could make use of him in the Coven. I mean, he might make direct contact with—you know—*him*."

"How right you are!" Nadine agreed in a great hurry. "See you this evening."

That finally got to the woman. She gave a coy little wave with three fingers, and hustled away. Nadine would have gotten up, obviously intending to go her own way, remembering all she had to do, but O'Flannery sat down again, heavily blocking her attempt.

"Laugh!" he muttered, grinning.

She laughed first, and seconds later, asked "What for?" But she knew. Whether or not the headwaiter or someone was watching them, hoping to listen in, she definitely wanted the owners of the Spa to know as little as possible. There were things about Lucifer Cove she profoundly mistrusted in spite of, or perhaps because of, her quick success here.

"Right!" she agreed when O'Flannery did not answer her purely rhetorial question. Still smiling, she murmured, very low, "I'm suddenly beginning to get the picture. This syndicate that owns the Spa, they let me make my little profit because that's how they learn the secrets of these poor devils. Then they must—what?"

"Blackmail them?"

"Of course. And when the victims, like Irena Byaglu, are bled dry, either emotionally or financially, they are driven to commit suicide, by some trick or other."

"Maybe."

She looked at him. He shrugged, leaned over her face and kissed her. His nose tickled her and she giggled though she found his kiss warm and marvelously strengthening. Meanwhile, she heard his whispered, "Change the subject," and did so.

"No!" she said firmly and aloud. "You know there's a meeting tonight and I'll be tired to death. Go find somebody at the Hot Springs."

"That change of subject was a very dirty trick," he whispered but staged a convincing fit of pique shortly after and stalked out.

Amused by the apparent ease of the deception on those in the dining room, she played it up alone for a few minutes by sighing impatiently, flashing indignant looks after the departed O'Flannery, and lingering over her coffee. She had just about made up her mind that her little performance was over when she made out Marc Meridon and Christine Deeth in the dim, half-dark banquette where Edna Schallert had sat half an hour before.

How long had they been there? How much had they heard? Perhaps nothing. They appeared so interested in each other they could hardly have had time to eavesdrop on her discussion with O'Flannery. But had they heard Edna Schallert's indiscreet talk just before she left the room?

No wonder Meridon remained so young, so trim! As usual, he had no appetite and was sitting there watching the beautiful Mrs. Deeth with that curious longing, almost lost look in his dark eyes, although it was understood by everyone at the Cove that the elegant, strawberry blonde head of the divorcée reclined on only one pillow—satin-slipped, naturally—belonging to Marc Meridon. She looked troubled now, her mind far away. Probably that was what haunted Meridon so much. In spite of his gentleness, his good looks and quiet air of authority, Nadine suspected his lovemaking was intense, if not violent. And if Christine Deeth was playing him for a sucker, she might find herself receiving a taste of that hidden violence.

Feeling she had played out her little comedy, Nadine got up to leave. Looking taller than her tiny height by virtue of her stance and the stark black and white colors she always wore, she prepared to give Christie and Meridon the faint, cold smile that suited the High Priestess of the Coven. It was not hard with Mrs. Deeth who always regarded a Devil's Priestess as a kind of female Mafiosa. It was, therefore, with a distinct shock that Nadine intercepted a look from Marc Meridon so intense, so stern and full of meaning, that she was left in no doubt that he had just issued her a direct order: "Persuade Mrs. Deeth to bring her crippled son down to Lucifer Cove! *Do it soon!*"

She did not stop to analyze her own reaction to this silent order issued by a man to whom she owed nothing except the morning's easy escape from Dr. Haupt. She only knew her knees suddenly buckled and she stumbled, catching herself just before she could fall. The headwaiter hurried to assist her and, feeling like a clumsy fool, she laughed and made her way out of the dark place with something less than her practiced grace. She still could not quite understand why she had so nearly fallen.

FIVE

"If I were the witch most people think I am," Nadine told herself with wry amusement, "I could guess what's in everybody's mind. Mrs. Deeth's, for instance. How does she hold onto Meridon? I could swear she's older than he is. Or if she isn't he certainly is well preserved. I must find out what his diet is." He apparently had a small appetite. He usually spent his mealtime, when at the Cove, watching Christie Deeth eat. In spite of the difference in their ages, if there was one, Christie Deeth unquestionably knew how to hold such a desirable man. High points to her for that!

It was not until Nadine was on her way up the mountain path to the temple that her last moments in the nave before the altar came back to haunt her. What an idiotic thing that had been! An aberration, but so real, so hideously real she was still aware of the horror that had burned through her at the sight of it. Then came the ridiculous part. She couldn't remember precisely *what* she saw there last night in the psychedelic light and shadow of the altar. It was as if her very soul burned in that awful cold fire.

"I hope I'm not inheriting all the horrors imagined by the suicidal old bags who come running here to escape from life."

This would be ironic because there were times when Nadine had found it necessary to resort to just such trick apparitions which, of course, substantiated Nadine's own predictions, promises and threats from On High.

She saw Edna Shallert's chalet along a path lined with slippery shale and pebbles and suddenly decided to clear up the air of Edna's annoying fantasies. Then there would be more time for that rest she always required just before the night meeting. And it would clear time for Christie Deeth, in case she took up Nadine's request to see her. It was still an "iffy" thing anyway. She couldn't quite figure the approach to Christie, with whom she had no rapport, no friendship, not even a gossiping acquaintance. She had once adopted a cat who had previously hung about Nadine, and that was a slight sore point as well. So far as Nadine knew, the woman had no faith in astrology, witchcraft, devil worship, or even the Tarot deck. What was the weak point by which to reach a woman like that?"

Nadine started along the path to the little chalet, staring idly at the distant peaks of the Coast Range shrouded in their hot afternoon haze, while she mentally examined all the facets of Christine Deeth's personality.

A clump of trees, dusty with summer dryness, briefly hid the chalet from Nadine's view and when Nadine had passed a particularly sinister and twisted cypress, she was surprised to find the strange, independent little tabby cat, Kinkajou, who had once followed her about the Valley, and then taken up with Christine Deeth. Now he was huddled on the wide step, obviously waiting for Edna Schallert. He pricked up his little pointed gray ears as Nadine's foot trod lightly upon a bit of smooth, layered shale. Then he ran to her feet and she picked him up, inordinately pleased at this mark of his returning respect. It could hardly be said to be a liking. He was such a fickle cat. He had never put up with her doings in the temple after the first few times. Perhaps he lost interest in the lighting and mask tricks by which she produced "devils" to scare or subdue her impressionable followers. O'Flannery claimed that Kinkajou, with his feline sensitivity, disapproved of her fake tricks. He liked the real thing, so the Irishman claimed.

"But he hangs around Christie Deeth now half the time," Nadine had protested, only to be assured that this proved O'Flannery's theory, because everybody at the Cove knew Mrs. Deeth was no phoney. Nadine had gritted her teeth, but without admitting it aloud, tacitly agreed that he had a point there.

Scratching Kinkajou behind the ears, Nadine went up the steps and knocked. For a few seconds she was afraid Edna hadn't come back yet, but the wide picture window was open and there were definite sounds inside. She heard something that could have been a woman talking to herself, or—and she hoped she was wrong—a woman moaning to herself. Nadine called out, added that Kinkajou was with her, and heard what must be her name called in a muffled voice. She opened the door and stepped into the pleasant, circular room which seemed to revolve around a hanging staircase. The furnishings suggested a snowbound alpine hut, heavy, warm, brightly colored, and comfortable—if the weather cooperated. It seemed wildly inappropriate on this bone-dry afternoon. Nor did Kinkajou like it. He wriggled in her arms and out of curiosity, if nothing else, she kept a tight grip on him, wondering what bothered the sensitive little fellow. Then she had a nasty thought. Edna had been talking about Irena Byaglu lately. Had that suicide virus hit her at this moment? It would be the one thing above all others that ought to excite Kinkajou.

"Edna! Are you here?"

"Upstairs, Miss Panos! Come up. But don't bring him. Whatever you do . . . don't bring him!"

"I'm not," Nadine called, bewildered. "I'm alone. Nobody came with me."

Whatever reply there was to this was punctuated by muffled weeping noises that Nadine heard with sinking spirits. She went to the stairs and started up with the squirming Kinkajou. "What are you up to?" She had never been upstairs in Edna's cabin. She popped up into a semi-circular bedroom where Edna, unaccountably, was huddled on the gaudy Indian blanket that covered her kingsize studio couch.

"I won't stand it another minute!" the woman cried with a note of hysteria, pushing one hand at Nadine with the fingers spread. "That cat! That horrible, soulless thing! He's—he's trying to communicate with me."

Nadine stared, at the same time losing her grip on Kinkajou who calmly, methodically, stretched himself out of her arms and leaped to the floor. Then he departed down the circle stairs, rapidly but with dignity.

With an obvious mental patient on hand, Nadine didn't know whether to give her attention to Miss Schallert or to follow and study the mysterious activities of Kinkajou. The whole thing was so ridiculous! Where had she gotten the idea that Edna Schallert would commit suicide? She was much too crazy!

"What's that in your hand, Edna? No, the one behind you." It was a claw-hammer. "Edna! Don't tell me you were going to hit poor Kinkajou with that!"

The woman, clearly overwrought, managed to calm herself under the flicker of scorn that she heard in the voice of her High Priestess. Slowly, shakily, she dropped the hammer on the bare floor, a sound that made Nadine jump, and then murmured huskily, "Do sit down, Miss Janos. On the bed behind you. I've got to recover. Funny. I used to like that cat." Her dull, gray hair fell forward across her colorless cheeks in a way what was hardly characteristic of the neat, if neurotic woman. She drew in her breath with a long sobbing sound.

"I can't help it. I know what it's trying to make me do. And I won't. I can't! Don't you see? It would mean my soul would go—to perdition."

"What is it that wants you to commit suicide? What is it you imagine is speaking through Kinkajou. Not my Lord Satan!" Nadine said quickly. "I can promise you that. You do believe in my powers; don't you? That I am in contact?"

Although the woman agreed, influenced as usual by a stronger will, she was clearly still in a state of agitation and finally got up enough courage to sneak a frightened look at the stairs, as if, thought Nadine, she expected Kinkajou to appear suddenly like the devil up from hell. It was so ridiculous it got on her nerves, making her angry, a dangerous luxury in her business.

"I am—I was a Catholic," Edna explained, moistening her dry lips. "I knew what we did here was evil. Worshiping My Lord—*him*—but he did give me happiness and love for the first time, and I just never counted the cost. But suicide . . . I tell you the voices get into my head. They tell me I've had it. It's time to join Sweetums."

"Sweetums!"

The woman made a nervous, embarrassed gesture. "It was my pet name for Gene Standish. So silly, but then, he was such a sweet, tender person to me until almost the last. You see, I know I've got to pay for his love and that's part of it. I know the voices are right. Only—what they ask is the greatest sin of all. And when I hesitate, that cat appears."

Nadine rolled her eyes ceilingward at such naïveté, or plain lunacy. "And I suppose the voices, or influences come out of Kinkajou."

"Sometimes. This afternoon it looked at me with an almost human face. The eyes, anyway. Burning."

Nadine was belatedly aware that all her muscles had tightened, marble-hard, while she stared at Edna Schallert. She started to speak, found herself without words and swallowed nervously. She had revealed none of this to Edna who, in the pause that followed, seemed to believe her whole experience was being ridiculed.

"I know it sounds so utterly fantastic. You must think I'm insane. But I had to tell you the way it affects me. Is there any hope? I'll pay anything. *Anything!* To be free of this dreadful haunting."

I will pay anything. Normally, these were the key phrases to raise the curtain on all sorts of glorious fireworks at the temple. But Nadine's reaction today was inordinately slow. She was still under the influence of that ghastly coincidence. Whatever her vivid imagination had conjured up last night because she was tired and worried, seemed to be contagious. The eerie thing about it was that even the woman's description hit it off perfectly. Nadine pulled herself together and managed by sheer self-hypnosis to instill confidence in herself and in Edna Schallert.

"My dear Edna," she began briskly, "we must offer up our prayers, our sacrifice, our best ceremony. We must win the Powers of Darkness back to our side. We have some excellent weapons, ceremonies that will delight My Lord Satan." Her mind was already busy on ideas that would be colorful enough to appease the appetites not of the Powers of Darkness, but of the idiots who believed in My Lord Satan. She walked to the big sliding glass doors that faced the north and opened first on the balcony directly over the hillside, where Edna Schallert had her meals, and then on the whole of the narrow north-south valley itself far below and currently shrouded in layers of heat and sulphurous smog. Somewhere in the desolate emptiness of the chalet's lower floor Kinkajou complained vaguely. He wanted out. "I must go and find him," she thought, but did nothing.

Edna Schallert didn't wish to throw difficulties in her way, and ventured in a gingerly manner, "I hope—that is, during the sacrifice, I won't have to be seen in the er—altogether, will I? I mean, my figure isn't the sort that—well, it wouldn't be any gift to the Powers, you know."

This idea was so ludicrous it restored all Nadine's former self-confidence. "Good Lord, no!" she assured the embarrassed woman, entirely unconscious of any irony in her slang. "We have girls we borrow from the Hot Springs for that sort of thing. The pay is not particularly exciting, but during the time they provide their services, they make excellent contacts for private arrangements with rich male members of the Coven. Or, in the case a male is used, entirely with his own consent, naturally, then these males make profitable arrangements with some of our older, wealthier female members of the Coven."

"Excellent contacts!" Edna repeated, greatly shocked. "I wouldn't quite put it like that. I mean, it is a religious ceremony, after all."

Nadine turned her head, concealing her smile. She had forgotten for a moment the woman's excessive prudery. How could the late gigolo, Gene Standish, possibly have found ways to tease and excite her? He must have had an uphill battle.

Kinkajou protested again, more loudly this time, and Edna looked toward the stairs in an absent way. "He used to be delightful. A real companion. Before that, he was attached to Mrs. Deeth. You never know where you will find him next. He really acts like a—a damned spy!" She threw out the word "damned" with an air of daring.

"He just wants to rove around. A typical male. I'll let him out. Don't give him a thought. I'll try and keep him away. But don't forget tonight's services either."

"Oh, I won't. I really won't! You give me new hope, Miss Janos."

Nadine had already started down the stairs when something Miss Schallert had said reminded her of a serious problem. She stopped, leaning her chin on a spiralling stair rail and asked thoughtfully, "How much do you know about Christine Deeth?"

Edna blushed a little. "I imagine you know where I met her. You know everything about us."

"Golden Gate Clinic; wasn't it? She had an unpleasant divorce and a nervous breakdown. And you were visiting there and persuaded her to come down to the Cove for a little final polish."

Edna said in her defensive way, "Well, how did I know she would take up with Mr. Meridon? Not that he isn't charming. But it certainly doesn't give her much chance to be with her children in San Francisco."

Bless you! Nadine thought—you've walked right into my problem with both feet. "I'm sure you're correct in that, Edna. And she misses the children terribly, especially the youngest, the crippled one. Too bad she doesn't join the Coven. She might have some of those wishes granted."

Surprisingly, Edna blurted out, "But she wouldn't do that. She'd be afraid."

"Afraid! She doesn't strike me as being afraid of anything. She practically runs the Spa, get anything she wants." Nadine remembered with a certain envy the effect Christie Deeth's faraway, abstracted attention had on Meridon. The woman's indifference was enviable. Nobody knew better than Nadine the importance of keeping one's personal feelings outside of one's work, and if one wanted to hold onto a man, one was careful never to weaken and to give more than one got.

"But she is afraid. I sometimes think you don't look closely enough into people's hearts, Miss Janos." She interpolated earnestly, "Not that you aren't wonderful at your work. But I think your usefulness with the Powers of Darkness would make you cynical about people's hearts. And Christine is torn between her love for Mr. Meridon and her affection for her sick son and her daughter, a girl about seventeen. Naturally, she'd be afraid to have them here."

"But why? Wouldn't that solve everything for her? We can promise not to corrupt them, if that's the problem. I don't believe in the corruption of the innocent, myself."

Edna looked at her in the annoying way that very sentimental women sometimes looked at her, as if she had missed something when the feelings were passed out. It was absurd, because no one was more sensitive to the desires and dreams of her Coven. It was one of the secrets of her success in the field.

"No, dear. She's afraid of something else."

Edna changed the subject to Nadine's annoyance. "Anyway, you've helped me a lot. I'm not near so on edge as I was. Before you came, I was imagining the most incredible things. Simply horrifying. But you know about that."

Since it was clear Nadine would get nothing more intelligent out of the woman, she left rapidly, reaching the curious circular room below and going to search for Kinkajou. She was still searching when there was a tearing sound followed by a crash and the unmistakeable squal of a cat. She rushed into a small front room that appeared to be the comfortable male sanctum of the late Gene Standish. The sliding windows here were open and a hole appeared to have been blow through the screen. She was crossing the room at a run when a reasonably human face peered in at her through the open hole in the screen. Startled and repulsed, Nadine screamed and then was furious at her own weakness.

With his marvelously evil smile, Dr. Erich Haupt greeted her. "Did I startle you? My apologies. But I was taking a little stroll through these so-intriguing hills when suddenly this little feline flew into my arms. He is yours?"

Nadine managed to control both her nervousness and revulsion and return his smile with a good imitation of her cool Priestess demeanor. It was always possible that Dr. Haupt might be of use to the temple in the future. In fact, the notion hit her now. He just might be of help in her present dilemma. Only this morning she had witnessed him come under to Marc Meridon's simple request. He could not be very fond of

Meridon. With this in mind she warmed to the man, in a business sense.

"How nice to see you here in my bailiwick, Doctor! You must stop by the temple and let me show you around sometime. You may find it interesting."

"I do not doubt that, Miss Janos. It would be a distinct pleasure. And this little eavesdropper? Shall he remain to witness our so-interesting discussion?"

She laughed. "Why not? He won't talk. I'll join you. Wait a minute."

It occurred to her that he ought to be suspicious of her sudden friendly manner after her anxiety to get out of his clutches earlier in the day. But on her way back through the chalet she decided that even if he guessed her motives were a matter of business, it would hardly matter. He seemed to be a very keen businessman himself. If was all to the good. She always trusted people who were ambitious and influenced by money. You could reach that kind, and understand that kind.

Curiously enough, Kinkajou looked quite contented in the prehensile fingers of the doctor. When Nadine reached for the cat he definitely retreated, making himself smaller, more secure against Dr. Haupt's lean body. Nadine felt a quick, stabbing little hurt that she recognized with amusement as a sense of rejection. She did not touch Kinkajou again, although she was acutely aware of the cat as she made her way along the narrow path beside the doctor.

"You were not happy with us this morning, Miss Janos. I wondered. It seemed a pity. We did what we could to bring you around, and there was always a chance of a relapse."

She was all sweetness. "And bring me around you did. I haven't had a headache since I left the hospital wing. But I had a great deal to do, preparing for tonight, you understand. Have you ever seen any of my ceremonies?"

"They are superb, and your knowledge of the occult, they say, is phenomenal. You would have been a very great success in the Germany of my youth." He saw that this didn't go over too well. Who wanted to be a great success in the late Third Reich? And more or less by accident, she thought, he stumbled upon a really captivating subject. "Are you a very close friend to Herr—to Mr. Meridon?"

She saw the chance to pry a little useful information out of him by a judicious hinting half-truth. "Not quite in your position. Mr. Meridon is one of your sponsors at the Springs, I am told."

"Now, I wonder who told you that curious information." While she digested this clever ploy, he bounced the conversational ball back to her. "I imagined briefly this morning that you were Meridon's—that, in fact, you were usurping Mrs. Deeth's place with Meridon. A dangerous game, I thought."

This was not quite what she expected, and it annoyed her, as did Kinkajou's inhuman gaze, as if he were trying to read her soul. "Why? Am I so inferior to Christie Deeth?"

He looked at her. The man might be sinister, but he was suave, and his ambitions, his successes with the Hot Springs were so like her own ambition for the temple that she could overlook the evil eyebrows, the cold Nordic eyes, the lascivious mouth.

"She is more beautiful, as you must be aware. You are not truly beautiful at all, Miss Janos. Or even pretty."

"Thanks." It was the flip, ironic interjection to be expected, but she was not really hurt. She knew there was something more to come, that would obliterate the insult.

"But then, I never knew a truly unforgettable woman who was pretty. Your watchdog, the Irishman, must find it endlessly fascinating to work with you on those devil worship meetings of yours. How I envy him!"

"Envy! But you must make a great deal more out of that Hot Springs bordello of yours than I do with the temple." She realized a second after she said it that this was tactless, when he had been so careful to compliment her.

Apparently he did not find the truth insulting either. He admitted with admirable frankness, "So true! A bit of a bore, nonetheless. The Hot Springs . . . the little after-dark Satyricon we permit—"

"Encourage."

"If you will. This involves the body. Your remarkable talents, they manipulate the human mind. Even the soul. What a triumph! Yes, I envy your Irishman. I wonder how you recruit your partners."

Open-mouthed at this audacity, she could only say the first thing that came to her mind. "Not partners. I have no partners." With a forceful edge that turned the boast into a subtle threat, she added, "I have followers." When he looked at her quickly, she smiled back, full of sunshine and innocence. But though she resented his assumption that she took in partners to share the profits from her unique talent, he had given her something to think about. By the time they reached the portico of the neat little Greek temple, she was wondering how Dr. Haupt's own talents could be utilized to the greatest advanaged. His corralling of sexual talents was not of interest to her. It was a subject, like drinking, where excesses left the participant helpless, unfeeling, a mere log. She needed the passions of her followers at their highest pitch. Otherwise, the visitations by the Powers of Darkness would have no shock, or mercenary value.

"Well, Miss Janos? What do you say? Have you found any use for me among all of—shall we say—my more dubious talents?"

She started. No wonder Kinkajou liked him. Their natures were oddly alike. How well Haupt had read her thoughts? With this talent he might be exceedingly useful in handling her followers, so long as he refrained from reading her own mind.

She glanced up at the doors of the temple, wondering briefly if anyone had gone inside since O'Flannery carried her out last night. There were too many complicated "scenic effects" that might be exposed to a prowler. Kinkajou's unblinking stare brought her back to the matter of Dr. Haup who was watching her with something of the little cat's intentness.

"I think we might talk it over, Doctor. On

the understanding that you do not recruit me to your Hot Nights at the Hot Springs."

His smile flashed and made the serious lines immediately afterward resemble a scowl. She wished suddenly that he had not smiled. Afterward there was a distinct, if brief, resemblance to Adolf Hitler in the narrow eyes, the stiff set of his face. It was a face she had seen duplicated a hundred times in Germany and in Hitler's own native Austria without the quick little shiver of repulsion she felt now, and dismissed, impatient at her own impressionability.

"Very well, if there is a place for you." She laughed. "And if you have a fondness for My Lord Satan."

"We will think of something, some way I might be of use to you," he said politely, adding, "I have some ideas." And he bowed in the stiff fashion she found absurdly anacronistic.

SIX

The tight, dungeon-like room where Nadine rested before the Services seemed especially stuffy that evening. Very much like a cat in a paper bag, she had always preferred these tight little receptacles where she could almost reach out and touch the walls on three sides, with a clear exit on the fourth side.

"If this keeps on," she thought, aware of a tight, binding pressure around her head, "I'll have to get an air-conditioner set up here."

But she knew her problem was not the stuffy room. It was the usual tension over her coming performance, the worry for fear something would go wrong. Tonight, for example, there must be special arrangements or "word" from the Nether Regions to stop Edna Schallert's suicidal tendencies. There were a number of other messages necessary to various Coven members. These could be fitted in as long as the expected titillation took place. To Nadine, the disgusting factor was that so many members came purely for the sexual frills, the nude body of the Altar Girl, the erotic prayers and litany to My Lord Satan.

She sighed, got up from the cot and stretched. All her muscles were sore, due, no doubt, to last night's fall. It had been stupid and careless of her, that fall. She still couldn't explain it.

When O'Flannery came into the room, reaching behind him and knocking as he walked in, he found her briskly going through a series of limbering up exercises. She saw him sideways from under her curved arm and smiled a welcome.

"How's the devil's handyman?" he asked in his lightly cutting way.

"Please! Handy Woman, if you don't mind."

He leaned over, peered at her under her too-thin arm, agreed solemnly. "Right. I hadn't noticed. Guess who's out in the auditorium at the altar, waiting for your okay."

She straightened, gave her figure the once more in the mirror, and wished she had dressed earlier for the service. She liked to make the proper impression. "Not Dr. Haupt! I don't want him getting too familiar with the props until he proves he has something to offer."

O'Flannery lost his good humor. He took this news more dramatically than she had expected. "You'll not be telling me that Hitler Reject is messing around here!"

She tried to be patient as she scrambled through her priestly wardrobe, searching for the night's appropriate vestments. "I said I don't want him messing around! Who is it you've got waiting for the okay?"

"They used to call 'em models. Or was it starlets? This one's the typical stringy haired blonde. One of those Meridon is always digging up. Good-looking body. Look well on the altar with all that candlelight mumbo-jumbo."

Nadine chose a robe carefully fitted in imitation of a Twelfth Century tunic, the material moulded to her slenderness, presenting to the beholder a black column, with deep, white-lined oversleeves. All her clothes for the temple were deliberately created for the special effects she achieved, those effects which looked so breathtakingly spontaneous. As she smoothed out the flowing lines of the tunic she became aware of the silence behind her. She glanced over her shoulder.

O'Flannery was looking at her with that special expression, half-admiring, half-animal, that she knew so well and knew too that she would be lost without it. She had a queer, aching desire to prolong this moment.

What would happen, she wondered, if she said "The devil with My Lord Satan!" and turned and went into his arms and stayed there, secure.

Until O'Flannery was consumed by desire for his liquor hangup, and Nadine got back onto her own endless quest for success . . . Forget it, Nadine. Forget the sex bit, the quiet life, the rest of it. Business is calling.

He took her shoulders, squeezed them under his big hands, lowered his head over hers and put his lips to the side of her throat, in the warm flesh just under the collar of her gown. He felt her trembling, knew that in spite of all her pretenses, her shrewish ways, her apparent indifference to any passion but success, she was his in that moment. Very slowly, and scarcely aware of the impetus that motivated her, she moved her head until her mouth lightly rubbed his lips. She kissed him, still slow to draw his passion, but with the steadily rising power by which she had held him through the past months and years. Since this always led to their making love and ended with O'Flannery describing himself as "drained dry by this vampire bat," Nadine was surprised at her own weakness now in this crucial hour, so close to the meeting of the Coven.

Her brain told her to get away, break this common-place physical spell which was merely a flesh weakness, a weakness she despised. But she made no resistance when he lifted her off the floor in that light, easy way which always gave him an added charm for her. She worked her fingers softly, deliberately over the tousled hair on the nape of his neck, drawing his head down to hers—

And in those seconds a shadow crossed the doorway. Nadine's delicious mood was broken and from the way O'Flannery muttered "Jesus!" she knew his mood was gone too. The thing in the doorway looked like a Halloween Trick or Treat, heavily disguised by a black Penitente's robe, rope sandals and a peaked hood with holes out for the eyes.

"One of my customers," Nadine murmured.

The Penitente spoke in a broad Sowthwestern drawl, "You all hidin' from me, Miss High Priestess Ma'am? Caint see a blame thang."

Nadine said in her slow, dignified "business voice," "You want guidance; do you not? Give me your hand. I will lead you to please My Lord Satan, and all things in his infinite world of pleasures will be revealed to you." She motioned O'Flannery to get out of the room and herself took the Black Robe's nervously extended hands and lured him further into the little cubicle. Blinded by the darkness after the faint light provided by the distant altar candles, the Black Robe blinked repeatedly. When O'Flannery passed him in the semi-darkness, the man tightened his sweaty grip on Nadine's hand.

"Cant see a blame thang. Don't leave me now, Miss Priestess Ma'am." He snuggled closer to her as O'Flannery passed behind him, trying not to indicate his presence or his departure. Such human qualities as sex or comradeship in the High Priestess were against the picture of the Untouchable she had conjured up for her followers. The fact that she presumably slept with no one except of course, her incubus, My Lord Satan, made her more easily adored by the Faithful.

Her Southwestern admirer, vainly trying to titillate himself and her by bringing his heavily robed body against hers in the dark, stiffened suddenly and tried to look behind him.

"What was that? Somethin' passed me. A kind of draft."

"Are you frightened, My Friend?" she asked significantly.

"You mean—"

"My lord and my lover," she answered with a certain honesty he couldn't perceive.

He was more scared than ever. "You tryin' to tell me *he* was in this room? The Old Nick himself?" He tried to remove his hood, the better to get a good look behind him, but failed. She saw to it that he remained too close to her to make the turn. At the same time, she took good care to remind him of his position in regard to this "god" of whom he required his favors. She knew the man was Buddy Hemplemeier who had done well in cattle and oil speculation and wanted to make a big splash in the New York Stock Market. Meanwhile, he was wetting his feet by way of the San Francisco Stock Exchange.

Nadine had early studied the Delphic Oracle whose ancient prophecies were double-gaited, and she followed the Delphic method in what O'Flannery called "your sneaky way." When she put on her show of calling up Satan to answer the prayers of her followers, she was careful to produce two replies: one in case the prayers were granted, one to explain any failure. Astonishingly enough, ever since she had come to carry on her trade at Lucifer Cove, a great percentage of these prayers were answered. It was only toward the ends of the lives of people like Irena Byaglu and Gene Standish, when their luck seemed to run out, that their prayers were unanswered. People like these unfortunate beings depressed Nadine who would just as soon see all of her followers happy and fulfilled.

"What is it you wish to ask my Lord Satan tonight!" she asked Mr. Buddy Hemplemeier in her cool, remote performer's voice.

"N-nothing now, Ma'am. That is—the Market's been so bearish, it works great for me to get the stuff at rock-bottom, but could it be bullish just a little mite? Long enough for me to unload the crap? Stuff, I mean to say."

"You must ask tonight. I can promise you nothing. We do not sell good fortune, as you must know." She tried to pilot him to the door but he was obviously enjoying his close proximity to her and she resorted to the old, useful ploy of muttering in a language unknown to this earth. She punctuated this with several appeals to "Satanus Dominus" which even Buddy Hemplemeier understood.

"Is—is he around here now, Ma'am? I better get going." He scrambled away from her as if he might catch a plague. "And you tell him I'll be real grateful. I mean moneywise." He stopped in the doorway, his black, peaked costume outlined by the candlelights in the main basilica of the temple. It was singularly inappropriate to the short, well-padded Mr. Hemplemeier inside the robes. "Thought I'd play it smart, Ma'am. You said three was my devilish contact."

"Satanic Contact."

"Yeah. Well, so I put three hundred shares of this stock—the bearish one I want to go bull— in old Nick's name. That is, in your name, Ma'am, for Old Nick. He will get the drift; won't he?"

"He will get the drift, My Brother in Satan. You must return now to your place in the temple nave so that your prayers will ascend directly to the black heavens and to My Lord Satan."

Meanwhile, she thought, concealing her amusement behind her aloof facade, "Let's all hope your bearish stock goes bullish. If I thought it would do any good, I'd pray to dear old Lucifer myself."

He trotted away, ludicrous in his robes, while she closed the door, turned on the light and repaired her stark, effective makeup which that near-seduction by O'Flannery had somewhat smeared. She was applying the touches that accentuated the hypnotic effect of her smoky blue eyes when she found herself abruptly in darkness.

The bulb had burned out, obviously. Impatient with this fresh delay, she knelt before the dresser and felt around in the bottom drawer for one of several extra bulbs. She was still kneeling when a breath seemed to cross her cheek very faintly. Remembering Hemplemeier's fear of "Old Nick" passing behind him, she smiled, but it was a queer, trembling grimace. The truth was that she had known it was only the Irishman whose passing caused that other draft. But the Irishman was not here now.

Or was he?

"Irish?" she whispered, but got no reply.

Definitely, someone or some thing had gotten in here with her. Furious over this unexpected cowardice she had discovered in herself, she abandoned the search for the light bulb replacement, got up and went slowly to the door, determined to show whatever power shared this darkness with her, that she was no longer afraid. The door gave her a few seconds' hesitation. The door knob was loose and required several turns before she could get the door opened. Meanwhile, her spine prickled with that uneasy sense of companionship behind her. In the second before she broke out into the hall, she flung out her arm, hoping to give something human —O'Flannery?—a good crack in the face with the sharp, platinum leaf design of the ring she wore. Nothing happened, and the opening of the door revealed that she had been alone in the little room.

"Am I beginning to believe my own tricks?" she asked herself, still in a state of nerves.

Fortunately for her sanity, the temple's main auditorium was now filled with her black-robed followers, and she had to concentrate on providing their entertainment. She could hear the shuffling feet, the buzz of voices muffled behind the black hoods, and, as always, these sounds revitalized her. She knew that Navidia Janocek would be fighting poverty and rats in some ghetto right now if there had been no stage lighting, no audiences like that one tonight before whom the 'nothing' Navidia Janocek miraculously became the hypnotic High Priestess, Nadine Janos.

She shrugged off that puzzling few moments in the dressing room, leveled her shoulders, and with that grace and dignity which were among her great assets, she walked along the hall toward the back of the dais where the altar stood. As she stepped around an ell in the hall and slowly mounted the dais, her entire congregation appeared before her, a mass of black robes with the ignorant, innocent, greedy, searching eyes all glistening from behind the peaked hoods.

Upon her appearance the temple lights with their high-placed little gloves dimmed to an eerie blue. The steady, rising flames that mounted from the twin silver candelabra on the altar were carefully placed to illuminate Nadine's face in the special and eerie way, deepening the shadows to attenuated triangles, making her eyes glow with an unholy light.

In the abrupt silence that had attended her appearance she wondered if anyone but she heard the very faint, distant sound of a night bird out in the moonlight as it flew in panic from some imagined danger. And what danger did it fly from? It seemed to her as she advanced silently to the altar that danger crowded her from every direction, but the danger was not the kind she was used to, physical, obvious: an attack by a disappointed worshiper; a rape attempt by a sufficiently aroused Hemplemeier.

But this evening, made hypersensitive by her experience at this altar the previous night, and by the strange little sense that some unseen presence had shared her dressing room tonight, she was inwardly nervous; although her outward look was as glacial as ice.

She raised her arms, began her chant which contained enough Latin to fool all but the scholars present, and the congregation picked up the litany, those worshipers with previous experience leading the neophytes. She had conducted this mumbo-jumbo so often she could go on and on while her active mind considered those eyes below her, all staring up at the altar, the candles and at Nadine. She had a sudden, fascinating idea.

Was Dr. Erich Haupt, with his flat-faced, petit-bourgeois look of Hitler, staring up at her from among those peaked black hoods? She had enough ego to assume he would be motivated by admiration for her success, and she was not one to discourage that. Which of these silly, greedy, hopeful people could he be?

She let her voice subside, sliding off into the

pregnant silence. It was at this point, as she reached out, taking the big silver crucifix, overturning and setting it securely upside down on its secret base, that she always glanced at O'Flannery, looming tall and powerful at the extreme right of the little auditorium, shrouded like the rest in his Penitente robe but with the hood on the back of his head so that his face was visible to those who looked into that dark corner. It was his nod and a play of fingers against the black of his robe that signaled her about the night's gifts, the offerings to the Powers of Darkness by those who wished their prayers answered by her intervention.

Tonight, for some reason—he had begun to drink, probably!—O'Flannery wasn't where he ought to be. It was disconcerting. She always felt just a bit uneasy when he failed her, as he occasionally did. At the same time she heard the little hiss of shock from many of the congregation who saw her replace the crucifix in its sacrilegious position and understood finally that their friends were right: This place did specialize in unholy rites. She was amused by the naïveté of men and women so selfish they sought fulfillment of every vicious, erotic or selfish desire, yet could be shocked by the position of a man-made object like this crucifix.

Because there was always such titillation over the use of a pretty and voluptuous girl as the immediate altar for these greedy prayers, Nadine staged the ceremony with the girl being placed in position later, thus prolonging the anticipation.

Now, the Eucharist of Beliol began. Two

Black Robes approached her, one from either side of the little auditorium. They carried silver chalices that gleamed and winked in the candlelight. The contents of these Nadine blessed, invoking the names by which a devil is commonly known in Christian society. The contents of the chalices were tonight a fruit and vodka nectar in which a hint of "acid" had been mixed to act as an aphrodisiac plus, if all else failed, producing a trip guaranteed to assure the drinker that he *had* enjoyed a successful encounter, whether he had or not. Usually by prepayment, three of the regulars and four others were picked at random from the congregation. But it was done in sevens. This made the act more exclusive, more sought after, and in the end, more remunerative.

The throng went down on their knees. Most of them, remembering childhood training in church or synagogue, closed their eyes or modestly stared at the floor. A few, to Nadine's secret amusement, were bolder and peeked up at Nadine, looking more impressive than ever, as she stood above them, raising her arms again to call upon the Powers of Darkness. Since she had no indication from O'Flannery as to the number of requests tonight, she used her usual tactics, making her prayers generalized in their demand, yet particular in application: "One among us, adoring Our Lord Satan, prays to you for—"

She was especially careful to pray for the "Peaceful Mind of Our Sister in Satan." That would be Edna Schallert.

During this time the lucky seven chosen for

the Black Communion had risen and shuffled to a place below the altar. They drank from each chalice. There was seldom a protest about germs, though each drank where the other's mouth had touched the metallic edge of the cup, raising his hood to do so. But Nadine was prepared, in case of that unusual occasion when some health nut protested.

Once, when the spell threatened to break because Edna Schallert drew back at this juncture, Marc Meridon himself had appeared quite unexpectedly and offered her a pristine white handkerchief. Nadine had recognized him by the few quiet words he spoke to reassure the woman, although he had not removed his hood. It was one of the few times that the rich Spa owner had joined her congregation, and since he asked nothing for himself, she assumed he was just curious.

Now came the pièce de résistance which, Nadine often told O'Flannery, was the real selling point of the whole Devil's Coven. The nude beauty who represented the altar in the final sector of the rites.

At a signal the worshipers came to their feet again. What Nadine referred to primly as the "music of the spheres" was carefully piped in, so dim, so dissonant, it was not at once recognizable. Spherical lights from the high beamed ceiling descended, flashing and reflecting myriad colors, from their many mirrored surfaces. This effect, as the tiny surfaces turned and twisted, worked wonders in hypnotizing those of the worshipers who hadn't been able to share in what O'Flannery called Nadine's Famous Stir-em-up-Cup.

When these effects were at their height, Nadine raised her arms once more, using her long, thin fingers with the practiced agility of an orchestral conductor, and two of her robed and hooded adherents, having previously paid for the privilege, bounded swiftly onto the dais behind her, bearing between them the supple body of the "stringy-haired" blonde girl whose flesh gleamed, sometimes pink and sometimes gold under the transparent black chiffon covering thrown over her to blend with the shadows that tantalized by their half-seen presence. She was laid upon the altar, her hair dragging over the side like a thin yellow waterfall against the black mahogany of the altar. The girl herself was not drugged. It was the one thing Nadine insisted on, that the "altar girls" should know exactly what they were doing, but the lights, the music and the scene itself were effective enough to subdue each girl's natural nerves and to produce the most erotic invitation in her body as it lay quietly while the Powers of Darkness were invoked over her erect breasts and ready flanks.

With clockwork precision Nadine led her congregation through its familiar steps, but there was an interruption of sorts which proved more upsetting to her than she had expected. During the moments when she called ritualistically upon "My Lord Satan, come to me, come to me, come to me . . ." she saw a movement from one of the two men who had placed the blonde on the altar. He was quietly, unobtrusively removing the peaked hood from his face. It was an act forbidden, and the man would not be allowed to perform in the rites again, no matter what payment he offered. It was difficult for her to see his face. There were the eyes of the entire Coven upon Nadine and she dared not turn her attention to this troublemaker.

Meanwhile, the still-masked Buddy Hemplemeier on her left, fulfilled his part of the show. He drew out black-painted bamboo sticks from his robe and dropped them in the empty chalice beside the blonde hair of the altar girl. The Coven generally separated now into male and female. There were often Lesbians in the "male" group, or females wanting to try the double-gait, as one tries absinthe or Speed or Big H, for the thrill of it. While these were drawing bamboo sticks in the hope of winning a go at the blonde, Nadine took the moment when the attention shifted from her to study the identity of the unmasked man. She saw and recognized the face at the same instant that the Coven saw the features of Dr. Erich Haupt, highlighted by the eerie shimmering glow that produced such an effect for Nadine.

But to the Coven, Erich Haupt presented the embodiment of the Century's most notorious criminal, Adolf Hitler. Panic endued in short order, and the blonde, the bamboo chances on winning her, even the possibility of each follower having his prayer answered, was forgotten. Tearing off their hoods, stumbling over their entangling robes, Nadine's congregation fled from the temple.

They had counted on and been aroused erotically by the possible appearance of a devil who few of them really believed in. But the architect of the Third Reich was another fiend entirely. *They could believe in his existence!*

SEVEN

Dr. Erich Haupt found the whole thing riotously funny, once the exodus had turned into a rout and Nadine was angrily cleaning up after the disaster. She was also telling herself that he wasn't going to get into her good graces, and her temple business, by this kind of practical joke. As if the Hauptian sense of humor were not weird enough, she was beseiged by the stringy blonde Altar Girl who kept following her around the auditorium of the temple, pinching her arm to get her attention but not lifting a finger to help collect all the abandoned robes and hoods.

When Nadine ignored the girl, she complained in a nasal whine, "They promised me a few bangs would be worth some contacts. All I get's the cruddy pay for a flopdown on your silly altar. Who pays me? Where's that big, Irish looker?"

With an angry swish of the last wrinkled, dusty robe, Nadine promised, "I'll pay you. And put your clothes on, for God's sake!"

"Look who's calling on God! Anyway, where'd I leave my clothes? Let's see . . . that little hole behind the altar. Hey, Mister, you're in my way."

Nadine was finally jarred enough to look up.

The sight was so ridiculous she found her anger evaporating in a laugh. The girl had turned and found Dr. Haupt blocking her way. He was looking her up and down, finding a normal satisfaction in the girl's sleek, unblemished body that shone in the candle light almost as bright as her hair. Oddly enough, Nadine thought, he was not sexually aroused by the sight of the girl. His interest was businesslike, and at brief seconds, rather clinical, as if he speculated on just how the girl would look, disjointed like a chicken fryer. The girl, on the other hand, studied his face with its sinister, historical resemblance, and as she pushed by him, she remarked in the most normal, incurious voice.

"You look familiar. Have we met some place?" Then she strode off toward her clothing.

Nadine remarked sardonically, "That will put you and your previous resemblance in proper perspective, *Mein Fuhrer*."

He shrugged, smiling, and took the robes from her. "We have an old Aryan proverb, 'You cannot win them all'."

She slapped the hoods across his arm and went after the girl. If you didn't watch these Altar Girls, they would steal your eyeteeth.

The girl wore so little when she was dressed, a mini-shift over bikini-sized panties, that she was dressed by the time Nadine reached the dressing room and since Dr. Haupt had followed them both, Nadine was not surprised when he offered to escort the girl down to the village.

"And it may be," he explained to the girl in Nadine's hearing, "that we can reimburse you for your failure to make contacts tonight at this temple."

Here he goes, Nadine told herself, making his bordello deals, and on my time!

"Do I look like the kind to empty bedpans?" the girl asked flippantly. "You're the doctor at the Clinic above the Hot Springs, aren't you?"

"But I do have certain interests in the nightly entertainment at the Hot Springs. It was that to which I had reference. One of our assistants, Ricardo Shahnaz, can give you your orders, suggestions, what-you-will. He has seen better days. The fellow is decaying, and at an earlier age, too. But he can tutor you briefly."

"Oh, well, that's a whole different can of peas. Sure. Include me in. And on the way down, you can tell me all the details of the couplings I hear a lot about. I heard from a gentleman friend all about some Romans on an island. Capri, I think. And about how they made it three or four at a time. That ain't easy, Man!"

"No, indeed!" said Dr. Haupt as they went off down the dark trail.

Nadine made a face, fanned out the strong cheap perfume of the girl, and half-decided to refuse Dr. Haupt any part in the temple. She wanted not a shred more of sex here than was presently provided. Her profits and her hold on her followers were both predicated more than sixty-five per cent on her followers' cupidity in business, or even health, a desire for a love to be returned. If she had no more to offer than the sex-oriented Hot Springs, then she would have no special place in Lucifer Cove. Besides, it was more degrading than Devil Worship. Anybody knew that! So let Erich Haupt keep his damned couplings and triplings out of her precious little temple!

She piled quantities of robes in a heap by the door, making a mental note to have everything cleaned in a hurry-up job outside the Cove before the next Coven meeting. O'Flannery saw to a lot of these details, or deputized people. Damn! Where was he now when she needed him so much?

She admitted after a surprised consideration of his absence that it was not entirely his usefulness with details which made her want him now.

"I need you, Irish. Me. The one who doesn't need anybody. I need you to fuss over me and call me Princess and make me feel like that 'adorable little girl' that homely little Nadine Janocek never was."

Was he still here in the temple, sleeping it off? It was an odd thing because O'Flannery almost never got that bad. He simply remained pleasantly under the influence of the brew he sometimes called in an ancestral brogue he affected, "The Good Irish."

Nadine walked through the hall to her dressing room, remarking that in spite of O'Flannery's disappearance, the temple was far from empty. It was like last night, and she had no intention of repeating that weird, hallucinatory fright with the resulting crack on the skull when she fell. She zipped off the Medieval gown, got into her long, high-necked black and white Chongsam that was split up the leg to her upper thigh, and achieved both her sensuous aura and the intriguing "concealed" look which puzzled the Cove's inhabitants and kept them guessing. Is was true that she had nowhere to go at this hour, except down to her suite at the Spa, but she was wise enough to know that she should never let down her image.

She knew she ought to check out the entire temple before closing. The two electricians, and the powerful, not-too-bright female who currently dabbled with the sound effects, had all shaken off the Hitlerian dust of the temple and vanished with the congregation. But she found that in spite of her frequent boast that she had courage, if nothing else, she had temporarily lost that too, thanks to her recent experiences here at the temple. In deference to her memory of last night's careless backward step, she walked sedately out, locked the door and went down the steps taking a deep breath of the pure, cool night air.

How odd to think that Lucifer Cove, with all its sybaritic and evil delights, was still entitled to those starlit heavens shared by the dull, puritanical majority of the world. She had long despised this majority, for its failure to go out and take what it wanted, or to work for the fulfillment of its desires. She considered the excuses of "decency" and "unselfishness" to be mere cop-outs. They were all hypocrites, this majority that settled for what it didn't want. In fact, she had built her entire success on this point of view.

This time when she looked back at her little temple it shone with pristine purity in the night light. No haunts and ghosts there. Savoring the night she went rapidly down the trail, rather glad now that the valley lights, high, pale, casting faint blue light, were always turned off early. It was good to have thrown off her weird, unaccustomed fears and to feel like herself again, master of her own destiny. Several times lately she had almost doubted herself.

On the little footbridge at the bottom of the trail she could see two people, obviously lovers, very close together, both dressed alike in what appeared to be dark Mao jackets and trousers. It was hard to guess which was the female until she reached the end of the bridge and heard the voices. They were both male. The older was complaining jealously about a rival. The younger caressed him, more or less absently, while looking off toward the Hot Springs at the north end of the valley. Then the two lovers melted together in one dark, thick shadow, making concerted groans and breathless gasps.

Nadine hesitated, wishing there were some other way to get onto the main street of the village without crossing the bridge. But she did not feel like wandering along the dry river bank in the dark, scratching herself, tearing her clothing, only to avoid the pair on the bridge. She stepped onto the loose boards of the bridge, her slippers making a gentle creaking sound which broke the pair of lovers apart, the younger man turning deliberately away from her to hide his identity, while the older man stared at her with what she read as an agonized plea. She had seen this reaction to her presence before and understood the plea. To the agonized man she represented the priestly intervention with his god, who was "My Lord Satan." Nadine slowed her measured pace, giving the man time to consider what she represented in future happiness, providing he made her intervention financially worthwhile. Having demonstrated the uses of the Devil Worshipers' Coven, she moved on, glad to be away from the vicinity of the pair. Having no sexual temptation that would not be understood in the most "normal" bedroom in the world, she could afford to despise the pair, including the wrinkled, agonized man who looked to her and her "master" for help. It was not in her job to provide sympathy, but merely the fulfillment of her Coven's dreams. Sometimes this required a little genteel blackmail applied to the younger of the two men but it worked in a great percentage of the cases.

By the time she reached the Spa she was physically tired, a pleasant kind of tiredness in which her muscles enjoyed their strong usage in the long brisk walk down the trail. She looked around once, remembering O'Flannery's remark about all those darkened house fronts, that they were like movie sets and that no one had ever inhabited them. Absurd as his claim had been, there certainly were no signs of life in those Tudor fronts at this hour.

"Some time I'm going to take Irish up on one or two of his wild ideas." *Irish, where are you, you idiot!*

Entering the Spa, she shrugged off this sign of her own weakness—and for a drunken, unreliable rogue like Irish! A new girl, a redhaired beauty, was still at the Reception Desk, perched on the desk itself, legs crossed with careless grace. It was the girl called Araby. She was carrying on a loquacious flirtation with Sean O'Flannery who stood behind the desk lighting a cigarette. As Nadine watched in the dark hall, speechless and white with the shock, he took the cigarette from his lips and placed it between Araby's teeth in what Nadine considered an exceedingly unhygienic way.

Silently, Nadine moved on, desperate to escape without being seen. To let herself be seen now would be to show herself as vulnerable, and when you were vulnerable, you lost all your power. It was her oldest rule. She was so anxious to escape that she turned too quickly, before she reached the wide, dark Jacobean staircase, and finding someone in the hall behind her, she took the only other route. A minute later, she found herself within a few feet of the indoor pool which was popularly referred to as the Blue-Green Room.

It was not one of her favorite places. The strange psychedelic colors made her seasick, and they were everywhere, from the pool waters gently shifting, to the walls and curved ceiling that gave the place its ghostly echo qualities. Even her footsteps carried, repeating the light, little sound over and over, pounding rhythmically against her ears along with the slap-slap of the pool waters. The waters gave off a moaning sound that unnerved her.

She kept moving slowly along the side of the pool, looking back over her shoulder and hoping against hope that O'Flannery would not come through here on his way to the Mirror Cocktail Bar with the beautiful redhead. What the Irishman did wouldn't matter nearly so much if only Nadine did not know for certain. Her ego, which ruled all her waking thoughts and most of her dreams, would allow her to imagine he belonged to her exclusively, if only she saw nothing that directly contradicted her vision of him and of her own power.

There were steps in the hall outside the Blue-Green Pool. Anyone making his way to that popular rendezvous of self-admirers, the Mirror Bar, would have to pass through this room, beside the pool. She moved further into the flickering blue-green shadows at the distant end of the pool, where it seemed to her the waters moaned and surged in greater volume. Water sloshed unexpectedly over her toe and instep. Unless, as Irish would say, the tide was coming in, there was no natural reason for these movements of the pool waters. They shifted like jello as she stared at them.

For the first time she gave all her attention to the pool. The echoes were extraordinarily penetrating. She began to wonder if a dog or cat had been trapped in here somewhere. The footsteps in the hall receded. Taking a short, quick breath, relieved that she had avoided a confrontation she dreaded, Nadine turned to the curious matter of the pool and its echoes. She followed the pattern of the blue-green tile around the pool toward the dim recesses in the far corner.

Someone was bobbing vaguely around in the pool, slow-motion strokes, curiously ineffectual. At least, it wasn't a suffering trapped animal. It was only a human being. And things were always happening to the clients of Lucifer Cove-

It was, she often thought, as if the Spa's clients became surfeited with all life's goodies, choked on them, on their own greed. And nothing remained for them but death.

"Who is it? Are you hurt?" she asked, a little shocked by the sudden sound of her own voice which came slapping back to her from every corner of the big room, like a ball bounced against a wall. "Who are you? Can you talk?"

The tile strip against the back wall was narrow. There was no room for a walkway here. She knelt on the tile as she reached out over the water, dimly making out the wet, gleaming features of a man's face, the wet black hair so tightly plastered against his head that she identified him by the shape of his skull. Ricardo Shahnaz, that sleek, dancing gigolo who had been managing the couplings at the Hot Springs. A dripping hand caught her fingers and the contact made her shiver. She freed herself with difficulty.

"Mr. Shahnaz, what are you doing hiding here in the dark? Do you know it is nearly midnight? You'll be needed by all those old ba—ladies of yours at the Hot Springs."

"Closer. Please . . ." His whisper was hoarse, unlike his usual, practiced tones which oozed a syrupy optimism. He used one hand on the pool's edge to hold himself in place, bobbing up and down in the seven feet of water, which was surprising because he was an expert swimmer, and Nadine had frequently seen him on the low diving board, either stretched out to show off his well-muscled body in its jock-strap trunks, or poised for a dive that would not take place until his audience was sufficiently aroused by the gorgeous sight before them.

"Are you sick?" Nadine demanded, adding cuttingly, "You look awful in these green shadows."

"Sick? If you only knew! But then, you probably do know." He moved up and down nervously, making waves. "Look behind me. Is anything in here with us?"

She studied the far end of the pool which was considerably brighter, with its streaks of blue and green, and the faint golden glow from the hall outside the Mirror Bar. "Nothing in sight. Are you hiding from one of those ancient females you've been diddling?"

He was roused to defend himself indignantly. "I never diddle females; they find me delightful. But no matter. All that is past now. I had an attack tonight. I have developed intense pains here. The belly. And tonight, I went black."

"Ulcers."

"As you say. But I am told it would take months of healing. They removed me to the hospital wing. I heard them talking. The great ox of a nurse and the surgeon. I am as good as dead."

He was merely dead drunk. He must be or he wouldn't be rambling like this. "Don't be ridiculous. Anybody who is anybody has ulcers. I've had one myself."

He pulled on her sleeve. "I hear something."

A man and woman came out of the Mirror Bar and talked in the hall. They were arguing. The woman, at least, was arguing about a phone call. For some reason the man was trying to persuade her to make the call. From their voices Nadine thought they were Christine Deeth and Marc Meridon, but it was apparent Ricardo Shahnaz, in his sick panic, thought they were monsters of some kind.

"I've been found. I thought I'd get away. I was clever. I got out of the hospital wing, but someone followed me."

Nadine was getting tired of these drug-induced fantasies. "Don't be so jumpy. What can they do to you? You're no innocent virgin to be raped. No female to be mistreated. What can you lose by being treated there?"

"No, no! I thought you were in on it. You see, they use us. People like me. As long as one can take it. Then, the minute one fails—it's the hospital wing. And next, the Cove hears that one is dead, poor soul. Sudden complications. And the funeral. The cremation. The end. Cremation! To me, of my faith, it would be a mortal sin. No. An immortal sin!"

She wanted to smile at that, but did not. She agreed privately that there was a modicum of truth in what he said, but the so-called victims, were invariably lechers, or murderers or bitches, or totally worthless characters of one sort or another. Few people mourned them, none investigated their deaths. And Nadine was not one of the few who would mourn them. She had better things to think about. Now that she had satisfied her curiosity as to Ricardo's identity and heard his drunken, or drugged tale, she was relieved when she could free herself from him. She scoffed at his fears and started way from him, along the tile.

"Don't! You are the Priestess. You can help

me. Protect—" He reached for her, barely missed the hem of her narrow skirt.

"Go back to the hospital!" she advised him. "Ulcers aren't something you can play with. You've seen enough of the debauchery at the Hot Springs. It certainly can't frighten you."

She had thought his ulcer incapacitated him, but his fear must be greater than she supposed. After a quick look around the pool's edge, he pulled himself up, dripping wet. Then, with a grimace of pain, he doubled over, groaning. Nadine considered these sound effects amateurish, but she was halfway across the room before it occurred to her that the man was genuinely suffering. She would have to do something. It was boring. She was tired. The evening's Coven meeting had been a disaster, and to cap it all, the infuriating O'Flannery was somewhere in this very building doubtless bedding down that redhead!

This idiot, Shahnaz, deserved whatever happened to him. But there he was, groaning. She swung around before she could talk herself out of it.

"Sit down! Where you are. Just sit! I'll get you some help."

He could do very little else. He really looked done up. When she looked out in the front foyer beyond the dark Jacobean staircase, no one was in sight. She wondered briefly whether O'Flannery had gone up those stairs with Araby the Redhead, but that would have to wait. There was nothing for it but to break up the interesting little dispute between Marc Meridon and Mrs. Deeth. She passed the poolside and found the pair beside the antique gold and ivory French Phone in the hall of the Mirror Bar. They looked around, startled at her interruption. She thought that though Marc Meridon frowned very slightly, Christie Deeth looked relieved. She explained rapidly, trying not to take too much of Meridon's time. In spite of his good manners she never took him for granted. He was the only person she had ever known who over-awed her by merely saying "Good Evening."

"I am sure Mr. Shahnaz is capable of taking care of himself," Meridon assured Nadine, but not entirely to her surprise, Christie Deeth urged him.

"Do go and see, darling. The fellow may actually be ill."

With his lips thinned dangerously, Meridon strode off to the blue-green pool. Christine waited. When Nadine started to speak, with an apology for having interrupted an obviously personal moment, Christie silenced her. She motioned in a conspiratorial way and a confused Nadine obediently went before her into the Mirror Bar. This was the only gesture of friendship the Deeth woman had ever made toward her and it was puzzling.

"What do you drink?"

Nadine was aching to know what this sudden cosiness would lead to, and anyway, it was too late for the hard, ruthless stuff, so she ordered a hot brandy with a twist, and then stood expectantly, flexing her fingers to relieve the sting of the hot glass. Bruce, the barman, was an extremely pretty young stud with a mass of black curls worn long in back but short enough on the sides to reveal the pointed ears of a satyr. Nadine had a strong suspicion that much of his other equipment was borrowed from the god he so much resembled, Pan. He gave her a contemptuous look which rather amused her. Sooner or later, she had no doubt, he would come crawling to her temple for help. The Devil's Priestess made it a point to provide mental, if not physical, assistance to almost any of the Cove residents. It added to her power and her self-satisfaction.

As Nadine nursed the hot drink, Christine motioned her over to a corner of the room, obviously intending to confide a secret. The room itself was always disconcerting to Nadine. She liked to picture herself in the theatrical lights and shadows of the temple, or making a grand entrance somewhere. But this bar was a room entirely paneled with mirrors so that no matter where she looked, she saw herself multiplied to infinity, a small, very thin young woman with noticeable, though not beautiful eyes and an otherwise ordinary face. It was the ordinariness she hated!

"Miss Janos, you can do me an enormous favor, if you will."

It figures! Nadine thought... She didn't invite me for a social drink.

Retaining the frigid High Priestess image which served as her perfect shell, Nadine rolled the hot glass slowly between her two palms, then sipped a moment. She was psychologist enough to note that her delay heightened the subtle marks of tension in this beauty who had everything the easy way and yet couldn't be happy. She said finally, "Of course, Mrs. Deeth. Anything I can do for you and Mr. Meridon."

Christie drained her glass rapidly and motioned to curly-haired Bruce. For one glittering instant Nadine thought this model of perfection, the only one of her kind at Lucifer Cove, was going to start on a bender. But no. When the young barman came along, Christie smiled, said "Sorry, no" and sent him back to polishing glasses. Like Nadine, she seemed to be bothered by the infinity of her own reflection in the mirror at her elbow. She blinked, turned her back to her reflection and then saw it again behind Nadine. It didn't make her any less jumpy.

Nadine reminded her, "How can I help you?" Some impulse, she was ashamed of later made her add, "I am rather well acquainted with Dr. Haupt at the Clinic. I understand you are bringing your little son down here for a short vacation. I'm sure you would find Dr. Haupt helpful. The therapeutic baths, and all." It was her own cruel little joke because she was fairly sure Mrs. Deeth did not want to bring her crippled and doubtless impressionable son to this place, and when she saw Christine's sudden pallor, she felt belatedly that the joke was a stupidity not worthy of herself. She had merely displayed a biting jealousy of the woman and at this point in her own success she no longer needed the crutch of jealousy. She was trying to phrase a change of subject that wouldn't sound too obvious when Christie put her hand out, spilling a few drops of Nadine's watered brandy.

"No. The opposite. Couldn't you—you have

ways of persuading people. And you do work for my—for Marc. Could you persuade him not to invite Toby here?"

Startled, Nadine had to correct one mistake that robbed her of her independence and pride. "Where did you get the idea I work for Mr. Meridon? I know the man only slightly. And he would certainly listen to you before he paid any attention to a comparative stranger like me."

"Miss Janos! If what you say is true, then you simply don't understand the situation. My little boy couldn't possibly be brought here. He might fall into the power of—of—"

She was so shaken, behaving so oddly, Nadine wondered if Christie Deeth were going off her head. She wouldn't be the first in the Cove to do so. Nadine made a quick gesture in the direction of the young barman but Christie seemed beyond caring about appearances. She did lower her voice but only because she was clearly afraid of someone overhearing her from the hall and the Blue-Green Room beyond. So things were not perfect between Christie Deeth and her lover!

"The truth is, as you may have guessed, I love Marc very much. And if my son were allowed to remain here for any time at all, it would seriously interfere with our—freedom of movement."

Good Lord! Was this the woman's purely selfish reason for excluding her son from the pleasure of her company? Nadine felt a growing disgust and wondered why she had ever been jealous of such a creature. "Mr. Meridon thought it would make you happy to have your little boy here with you. It looks as if he guessed wrong there. If you are done with your drink, so am I." She set the glass down on the nearest gold mosaic cocktail table and started away with Christie's desperate voice calling after her.

"You simply refuse to understand. It's for Toby's sake. For Toby—" She broke off so suddenly Nadine looked up, wondering.

Marc Meridon came slowly into the bar. He looked tired, but his mouth was gentle as he held out one hand to Mrs. Deeth. "I'm sorry. I didn't mean to be so long. But I thought something could be done for him."

Nadine's heart felt as if it had been squeezed between cold fingers. "Was it so serious? I thought Shahnaz had an ulcer. Can't he go on up to Monterey or down to Santa Barbara for treatment? He seems to dislike the Clinic here at the Hot Springs."

"Yes. Why not, Marc?" Christie put in unexpectedly.

But Marc shook his head. "Too late, I'm afraid. The man has a history of heart murmurs, or some such thing. He died as Dr. Haupt's men lifted him onto the stretcher."

While Nadine was digesting this, Marc made a quick movement, and rushed past the startled Nadine who swung around in time to see Christie Deeth unaccountably fall in a dead faint.

EIGHT

The most impressive aspect of Mrs. Deeth's curious collapse was Marc Meridon's deep concern for her. While Nadine stood there with eyes narrowed thoughtfully, considering this unexpected development, Meridon looked up at her. She could never remember having surprised that special look in his luminous dark eyes. There was a dreadful suffering about it, an anguish that baffled her. Because his concern was so out of proportion to Christie's simple faint, Nadine found herself annoyed, wanting nothing so much as to keep from getting involved. There were too many raw nerves exposed, and in an odd way, they embarrassed her.

Nerves are stupid, she thought. They destroyed people. You couldn't afford to let them rule you. But she did not say this aloud. Other people's nerves were of great use to her.

"A drink, quickly," Meridon ordered Nadine, but the look of deep concern had not left his face. He appeared subtly older and Nadine wondered why she had always thought him so young.

She turned, reached for the glass held out by the startled young barman. She sniffed the glass, and as Marc reached for it, she shook her head. It was one of those insidious and potent House Specials which put newcomers into a frame of mind where all inhibitions were broken down and tossed away. Christie Deeth hardly needed that! Nadine handed the glass to the Barman Bruce. "No. This is a mixture. You want water for Mrs. Deeth."

The barman impudently refused to take back the glass until Marc shot him a sudden, piercing look that he could not mistake. He hurried away, but before he could get the water, Christie moved in Marc's arms and opened her eyes. Nadine watched her, puzzled. There was certainly love, and passion too, in Christie's expression as she saw Marc. Why then the flim-flam about being afraid for her son?

"What a stupid thing for me to do!" Christie tried to get to her feet but was prevented by Marc's gentle, persistent hold. "Really! I'm perfectly all right. It was that last drink. I guess you'd say I blacked out. Wasn't that so, Miss Janos?"

"Absolutely." Then Nadine intercepted one of those quick, unexpected glances from Marc, coughed and added in a hurry, "That is, it was just one of those things. Sometimes one drink will do it." She was only occasionally perceptive about personal danger, but being conscious of Marc's attention, she had a sudden inspiration. "Mrs. Deeth, believe me, I know about these things, like one simple drink that hits you. The answer is exercise. Don't you see?" Marc's mouth looked as if it would harden into disgust at this, but he was watching her narrowly. He must have a clue that Nadine just might help him. She obliged, rather proud of her own skill. "You'd be told the same thing if you were sick or overworked or crippled. If you'd broken your ankle and it was repairing, you'd have to walk on it eventually, to strengthen it."

Nadine could see that she had reached Christie who was too dazed to find this a rather crude lead-in to her son's problem. But Marc's expression of disgust—he had clearly understood the insidious connection—lightened considerably as it became evident that Christie was reconsidering the all-important matter which had driven a wedge between her and her lover.

Christie sat up, putting her hand gently over Marc's. "There may be something in what Miss Janos says. If I thought Toby would be safe here, we could do some walking together. And it might be better for him than the city, with all the traffic, and the crowds." She gazed up at Marc's face with that outgiving love which Nadine had sometimes seen on a human face like O'Flannery's at odd moments when he was happy with her. It was a haunting look because it had always made Nadine vaguely uncomfortable when directed at her, because she didn't know how to respond to it. In her artillery there was no possible response. She supposed it was some facility she was born missing. Like sight, or hearing.

It was only after she left the lovers and was going from the Gold Corridor through the blue-green room housing the pool that she wondered why, if Christie Deeth loved Maridon so much, she made such a fuss about bringing her boy to Lucifer Cove. If she was afraid the child would be corrupted by the Hot Springs, she didn't have to go there herself. There was no reason why a boy of ten should be brought anywhere near corruption.

The waters of the pool swayed gently. She glanced down, saw for a brief second the glossy, well-oiled body of Ricardo Shahnaz floating face up, his black-olive eyes staring at her. She closed her eyes, looked again. Nothing disturbed the softly swaying waters. From the blue-green waves in the mosaic pattern of the ceiling, the "slap-slap" came echoing back to her.

"I need sleep! I'm beginning to imagine things."

But her pace was more rapid now. She couldn't get out fast enough. It was a relief to find no one on the staircase in the hall beyond. She rushed up the stairs and found herself running by the time she reached the door of her suite. While unlocking her door, Nadine glanced along the hall to the door next to hers. The room was one in which that former member of her Coven, Irena Byaglu, had hanged herself from a ceiling beam. Irena's body was discovered by Christie Deeth, who had the south corner suite just beyond, and the suicide's suite was now occupied by a pair of adulterous international film stars.

The stars were at one of their battles now and as Nadine opened her door, trying not to wish she would find O'Flannery inside, the wall was shaken by a hard object that shattered, with many tinkles of broken glass. Nadine laughed in spite of her depression.

"Good bye, Mantel Mirror!"

There was a male bellow, followed rapidly by scuffling sounds, and a series of little shrieks

Nadine recognized as the prelude to their usual sado-masochistic love scene. Fortunately, after that, there would be a long silence until midmorning when the pair returned from their Hot Springs revels to sleep through the day.

While Nadine was showering, the movie pair went out after slamming innumerable doors. With any luck, Nadine hoped, they would wear out in double-quick time and either string themselves up like poor Irena, or wind up on a slab in Dr. Haupt's little clinic.

Eventually, there was a graveyard silence and Nadine crawled between the crisp, cold sheets with a contented sigh. She had begun to feel the reaction of the evening's excitement. Even the back of her head ached, more or less in sympathy with her general state of keyed-up nerves. She had noticed on some other occasions that the more tired she was, the less she could sleep. She looked at the silver box on the night stand. Her name was engraved on the lid, the lovely name she pretended to be, but there were times, like tonight, when she was particularly overwrought and the lovely engraving subtly changed into that ugly, dull Navidia Janocek. There was an assortment of drugs in the silver box. Some she recognized. Simple Seconal, and Nembutal or Demerol. She wasn't quite sure. And the local "acid" preparation, and dexadrine. The old witch-woman who ran the Cove's Pharmacy and Gift Shop made up the drugs with the liquor used in the temple's "Communion." Nadine wanted no part of it, or of anything else that robbed her of her power to make decisions, and run her own life.

But the silver box also contained aspirins, and she was grateful for that. The silver box and its powerful contents were a gift from the management to each of the Spa's new clients. It had always seemed to Nadine a cynical gift, and doubtless it proved an opening to a dangerous future, but that was *their* problem. Not hers. She made it a point not to touch the drugs, no matter what the temptation. Tonight it was an almost insurmountable temptation.

Half an hour later when she was in the middle of wondering whether she would be awake all night, she fell asleep. She woke up briefly at six the next morning with the sun pouring in through her east windows, and she stumbled sleepily over to close the blind. It promised to be another hot, smoggy day, with considerable help from the Hot Springs where smoke was pouring out of two of the disposal stacks. Closing the windows and then the blind, she stumbled back toward the bed trying not to shake herself out of that pleasant semi-conscious state that made it possible for her to return to sleep without quite having been awake.

She was startled by the sight of O'Flannery, asleep in the chaise longue, all his length of limb somehow crowded onto the fragile, satin-cased chaise. She was halfway across the room before she realized he was awake and watching her interestedly from beneath his lashes. Her pride nudged her to pretend she had not seen him, but the devious little second thoughts which had often been of great value to her, reminded her now that she must play it cool about him and the redhead.

She pretended to see him for the first time, grinned, and going to the chaise longue, leaned over and kissed him, missing his mouth when he smiled up at her. His big hands reached up, fastened into the nylon chiffon of her gown and squeezed, warm and reassuring, around her ribcage.

"Hello, Princess." He moved her back and forth between his hands, exactly as she would play with a cocktail glass. It excited her in the old, delicious way and what she wanted most at the moment was an escape from the insidious questions of last night. It was nice to be in Irish's hands, figuratively and literally, if only for this brief time of love. She let herself be drawn down to him, then down to the thick white shag rug.

All the painful strength of the big Irishman crushed her flesh in upon her small, brittle bones, smothering and possessing her in that special, brutal way which would end, as in all their encounters, with her literal containment of his strength, his masculinity. She had never said so, but she knew that this was the secret of many male-female couplings, and only the tired, drained males seemed not to realize it.

A few times Irish had called her a vampire and she pretended pique, had to be pacified and flattered, but she thought it remarkably observant of him, all the same.

Late in the morning, Nadine and O'Flannery had breakfast in her suite and who should come up to remove the tray and roll away the trolley but O'Flannery's redhead! It took one of Nadine's most difficult performances to greet the rangy beauty with any kind of politeness. She was remembering that O'Flannery had very likely come to her room and made love to her directly after leaving Araby. And if she let him know it, she would have to keep up the jealousy act which cut her off from him and left her completely alone. It was an effort, but she managed to retain that aloof, Devil's Priestess expression while Araby and O'Flannery exchanged small talk, as if they had nothing to hide from her.

"I'm all over the place today," the girl explained when Irish asked her what she was doing working out of Room Service.

Nadine thought cattily. She probably does a lot of working out of Room Service. . . . But she was wise enough not to reveal her natural talent for cattiness aloud.

O'Flannery persisted. "Why the slave labor? What happened after you closed up shop last night?"

Nadine's ears pricked up at this. Was it possible she had been too suspicious last night?

Araby laughed and shrugged. "I went to bed. What else? You don't think they're going to get me to contribute this fair white body to Old Haupt and his Jolly Jammers? Believe me, Boy, I had no particular use for Greasy Shahnaz, but the poor devil's bought it just a little too fast to suit Yours Truly."

"What do you mean?" O'Flannery asked in an odd, tense voice.

Araby rattled dishes and got the trolley moving with a good deal of squeakiness. "You didn't know? Damned fool had ulcers and for some reason, couldn't get up the guts, or money to leave here and go into a decent hospital. Topping it all—but Her Priestship can tell you more about it. She was there. Rough business, wasn't it, Miss Janos?"

Nadine was not immediately troubled over the attention this brought her from O'Flannery. It was the gradual change in his expression as he stared at her, from surprise to doubt, to suspicion, that made her flare up in quick self-defense.

"He told me he was sick and I called for help. He had a bad heart. I didn't see him die, but it was a heart attack."

"Then how did you know he died of a heart attack?" O'Flannery asked sharply.

Araby looked from one to the other of them with curiosity. Nadine had a notion the girl was genuinely surprised at the undercurrents here. As for Nadine, she felt herself to be in the right and therefore could afford to take a lofty tone.

"I know only because I was told so, by one of several men who saw him die just as he was lifted onto a stretcher."

Irish said nothing for a few seconds. Nadine didn't feel altogether at ease during that silence, and yet she couldn't think of anything concerning the death of Ricardo Shahnaz for which she blamed herself. He spoke finally, to Araby who was rolling the trolley to the open door.

"Did you know he had heart trouble?"

"No. Nor care. What is all this, Irish?"

So the Redhead called him "Irish!" Nadine added her own snappish, "Yes. Get to the point, for God's sake! What difference does it make whether he had a sudden attack, or whether it came on after all that sex-focussing he's been up to at the Hot Springs?"

"Well," Araby shrugged, "he focussed sex once too many times. I can't say I wept salt tears when I saw them shovelling him into the incinerator, or whatever you call the damn thing!"

"What!" Nadine and Irish exclaimed together.

"You mean you didn't know? And you two have been here practically since the dawn of creation?"

Nadine sat down abruptly. Her knees were giving up too often lately. That weakness unnerved her even more than the implication of Araby's casual remark. "They can't—I mean, there have to be licenses. Crematories need all kinds of permits."

For some reason this annoyed O'Flannery out of all proportion. He shouted, "Don't be so God-damned dense! Everything else is here. Why not a garbage disposal for humans?"

Nadine was remembering that moment in the hot, smoggy dawn when she saw the black smoke over the Hot Springs. She didn't realize how expressive of revulsion her face could be until O'Flannery with one of his sudden, mercurial changes of mood, reached out and grabbed her arm.

"What is it? What are you thinking about?"

"I saw Shahnaz' body burning this morning."

He dropped her arm, unable to hide his shock. "How?"

She explained what she had seen at the window. Araby shuddered and then, as if only physical action would wipe out the picture conjured up by Nadine's graphic words, she rattled the trolley into the hall, bumping into someone just beyond the door. "Sorry, Mister. Garbage Detail retiring as ordered."

O'Flannery glanced at Nadine who was nervously repeating, "I saw it. I actually saw that fellow burn. Only I didn't know it."

"You don't know it yet, Princess. All you know is, you saw smoke. And anyway, the poor bastard was dead. Araby was witness to that. What does it matter what happened to his body now?"

"But he hated it. His religion. He considered cremation a sin. He told me so before I went for help. He'll go to Purgatory."

It was not like O'Flannery to jeer at her when she was this upset, but for some reason he seemed to find this inordinately funny. "Princess, you'll be the death of me, sure you will! The guy was rotten. He corrupted and destroyed half the population of the Cove. And you think he'll go to Purgatory just because somebody burned his dead body! Besides, Baby, you're the High Priestess of Purgatory, and all that jazz. Just say a prayer to the devil for our precious Ricardo's soul. It would take a bit of doing, to save that soul. But I wouldn't put it past you."

"Nor would I," said Marc Meridon in the doorway as he knocked belatedly on the panel of the open door. He smiled, the winning, apologetic smile that always got Nadine. "Forgive me. I couldn't help overhearing. But I do agree with you about Miss Janos' talents. I wonder if I may speak to you alone, and very briefly, Miss Janos. About some possible worshipers at your altar."

This was promising. She became all business. "Not my altar," she reminded him with just the proper note of gravity. "The altar of My Lord Satan. Would you like to talk in here? Mr. O'Flannery was just leaving."

O'Flannery was still in his terry cloth shower robe with nothing underneath, and as the Irishman got up, Meridon laughed, remarking, "That seems a bit premature. I'll wait for you down in the Rose Salon."

When he had gone, O'Flannery went to the door, peered out into the hallways with a scowl, and then slammed and locked the door. "No accidental eavesdropping now."

"Never mind that. Help zip me up like a darling." She had raced into a pair of black and white hostess pajamas spectacularly sprinkled with cabalistic designs.

He did as he was told, jerking her this way and that while he pretended the zipper was stuck. She knew better. He always acted like this when he was jealous or she had provoked him in some way. He reached the neckline of her robe, and rubbed his thumbs along her neck with such force she cried out.

"What are you so mad about now?"

"Mad?" he echoed. "Who's mad? You go along, My Precious Little Monster, and wheedle your way into that fellow's good graces. Suck up to him. Maybe he'll get you human sacrifices to play with up at your sacred temple. Sacred to Evil, and Rottenness, and Corruption!" With each name he gave her neck a nasty little twist.

In some subtle way it amused her. He must care very much, in order to behave like this. Her reply was ice-tipped.

"Don't be so silly! You talk like a religious fanatic. Go tell it to a priest." She began to work up a certain amount of self-justification. "Did I ever corrupt anybody who wasn't corrupt before? Did I ever make anybody evil? I mean personally—me—make them evil?"

"Don't quibble. You'll spoil your fake eyelashes."

That practical note made her laugh and she felt she couldn't lose her temper with him, no matter what outrageous thing he accused her of. He gave her neck an extra wrench that made her choke, but before she could gouge him in the groin and release herself, he said in that tone she always recognized as worth listening to, "You go suck around friend Meridon. And I'll just go back to reading all about the body-snatching business."

"The what business?" That pierced her cool superiority.

He grinned but without humor, making her more than a little uncomfortable. "Why not? It's too unbelievable for the headlines; so the papers are sneaking it in on the gossip strips. But it's going on, all the same."

"What is going on?" She turned, wide-eyed, staring at him.

He looked down at her with one of his smug, know-it-all smiles.

"I'm not dredging this up to impress you, Princess. It's happening all over, with slight emphasis on Hollywood Graveyards. Stealing bodies of dead—and I may say—decaying—movie stars, for purposes of devil worship."

He really had flipped! "All right. All right.

You go back to your gossip columns, Irish." She extricated herself with a neat twist, and patted his arm consolingly. "I leave you with your decaying movie stars."

She went to the door, unlocked it, and walked out laughing. What an imagination Irish managed to cultivate, and he hadn't had a drink in hours!

NINE

All the same, Nadine wished Irish had kept quiet about his hair-raising graverobber tales. They had the authentic ring of horror, the kind that rivals in her field of deviltry had tried on her for years. Usually, it was the tired, beat-up old story of the medium who called on the dead once too often and one dark and stormy night the dead really appeared. That produced the wrong effect on Nadine who simply replied that she would like nothing better than such an event. It would increase her business.

But as she took the wide, dark staircase slowly, step by step, remembering the importance of her outward image, she did wonder what Marc Meridon wanted to say to her. She didn't fool herself into thinking he had suddenly succumbed to her feminine charms. There were too many beauties that Meridon and the other investors—whoever they were—had corralled for their use here at Lucifer Cove.

Caro Teague, the pretty receptionist who had taken the sexual leavings of Ricardo Shahnaz after he obliged the women at the night revels, came up the stairs at the same time. She was crying silently, the tears still streaking her face. As she passed Nadine on the landing, she stared, making no friendly sign whatever in reply to

Nadine's greeting which had been a subdued though ironic "Good morning." Nadine did appreciate the girl's feelings, but for some reason, Caro was acting as though the fellow's death had been entirely her fault. No matter. Caro ought to know, as Nadine had early known, that a place like Lucifer Cove with its pleasures, had its unpleasant side. Everything in life must be paid for. This was especially important to Nadine's profits in what O'Flannery often called her "Devilish Business."

When she came to the Rose Salon which was an elegant room between the stairs and the Reception Office, she slowed her stride, stood tall, and made an entrance into a room which had obviously been designed to make a woman look her best. The rose lights, the satin-striped paper with its flattering and youthful pink cast, the carefully chosen furnishings, all were a delight to women when they first arrived at the Cove. Much later, when, as Nadine had often noticed, nothing could save these people from showing the effect of their excesses, they avoided the Rose Salon. Perhaps it aroused too many poignant memories of those first deliriously exciting days when they thought they could enjoy any excess of pleasure with impunity. If their pocketbooks did not betray them by emptying magically, and people like Araby and Caro and Shahnaz did find other ways of paying for their stay, then the free use of drugs and sex in all its ramifications managed the job. The body eventually betrayed the Cove's clients, even if their wealth allowed them to enjoy their hedonistic pleasures for an inordinate length of time. Cynically, Nadine refused to allow herself to pity them. They could always leave; couldn't they? *Then, why didn't they?*

She was frowning over this thought when she stepped into the Rose Salon with her head up and her body carefully controlled to preserve the dignity that was so important to a small woman with a taste and talent for power. Marc Meridon stood across the room, smiling ruefully at the broken wing of an alabaster statue about a foot high.

"Disaster?" she asked lightly as she went toward him. The breaking of the statue gave her an excellent psychological advantage; since it placed him in an apologetic position, and he couldn't over-awe her, as he often did.

"I'm afraid so. It slipped out of my fingers."

She looked at it in his hands. It was the figure of a beautifully muscled male, an angel obviously with huge wings, one of which had been neatly snapped off. The right knee of the figure was bent, the left leg balanced behind him as if he were caught and preserved in alabaster at the moment of mounting some elevation.

"What is it supposed to be?" she asked and then saw from his flicker of surprise that he had thought her better informed.

"It is someone's conception of Milton's Fallen Lucifer."

Comprehension dawned slowly. "Oh. Then he is in the act of being thrown down the steps of heaven?"

Meridon considered the statue. "Quite the reverse, I think. You see the raised fist? He is trying to climb up to the throne of heaven. To conquer it, I think, or all the good that it represents."

"With his fist raised?"

"Why not?" His dark eyebrow arched in that expressive way he had. "Isn't that the history of nature? All weak things die, disintegrate, but the strong, the clever, the persistent, the intelligent survive . . . by preying upon the weakness of those other objects in nature. . . . Do you understand me?"

She studied the delicate statue. "Well, I don't think it's very clever for God's evil son to shake his fist at his all-powerful Father."

He smiled, ran one slender finger over the broken wing. "But even if Lucifer is God's evil son, he has his Father's powers, has he not? I mean, being God's son, even though he is disinherited."

She was surprised at his quaint sense of humor. All this ridiculous rehashing of medieval legends! Perhaps he'd been a scholar before he became so rich.

"I still think he would do better than wave his fist. He could use more subtle methods, like—" She looked around, shrugged. "—like corrupting God's other children." Then a sense of the silliness of this conversation came over her and she laughed. "Or do we sound like an incredibly dull pair of theologians arguing how many angels can fit on the head of a pin?"

He laughed, but reluctantly, she thought. "I'm afraid we do. Will you promise not to betray my secret?"

"Your secret?"

"That I am incredibly dull."

She said with a slight irony, "I wouldn't describe you that way. Your secret is safe with me, Mr. Meridon."

"Thank you." He put his hand out as if they had made a compact. She thought of his touch with a certain amount of erotic pleasure. She had admired and been curious about him, and secretly investigated him for such a long time. But oddly enough, when she put her hand in his, she was conscious of a dreadful sadness, a depression that crept through her flesh and into her bones like a contagion. She thought furiously, "He is hypnotizing me some way, and I won't let him control me like that. What is it to me if he's had an unhappy youth? Or whatever other excuse he's dug up."

She shook off this cold tension to suggest brightly, "And that's why you called me in for this little conference? To alibi the Case of the Broken Lucifer?"

"Not quite. Although I may need any alibi you will provide Miss Janos, when the housekeeper demands to know what happened to her precious alabaster."

"Glad to oblige. Any time." Still puzzled, she turned to leave. The entire interview had gone very oddly.

"Don't go, Miss Janos."

This time there was a subtle distinction in the way he spoke. No hint or plea for understanding. The steely confidence that had always existed below the quiet exterior of Marc Meridon had returned to his voice. It was not a request but a nicely veiled command. She stopped, looked around, wondering if, just once, she would surprise the real look—whatever that was!—on Meridon's face. She did not surprise it this time, either; unless his soul was mirrored in that gentle, dark-eyed young face that returned her gaze now. And this was not quite the face she had seen a few minutes ago either.

She did not want him to think she was intimidated by his command and asked coolly, "Yes? Something else?"

"I'm afraid we have not talked about the matter of business that brought me to call you in." As on several other occasions, she caught faint traces of an accent, or maybe only an inflection that was foreign. But she could never pinpoint his native land. He motioned to a stiff, exquisitely uncomfortable Louis XV occasional chair with a pad of figured pink brocade. "Do you mind?"

He really did have a remarkable nerve. Or maybe he was just used to buying his own way with people. But though he might run the lives of the rest of the Cove clients, he had never bought Nadine Janos. Whatever her ambitions, and however much she welcomed money, her passion for independence ruled her life. It was this very suspicion of him that had sent her scuttling over Northern California to track down information on Marc Meridon. Her undercover job, of course, had been a real bomb. It was remarkably difficult to find out anything about the man, except that he had a good deal of financial influence.

Nadine gave herself a minute of time by shrugging and appearing to consider his question, in order to save face. "I've no objection," she agreed with a glance at her wristwatch to indicate that her time was valuable. She sat down, and always remembering to play up her independence from his orders, she seated herself comfortably, crossed her pajama-clad legs and said in her professional voice, "Was it my official capacity that you wished to consult me?" She was surprised to realize, after she heard her own words, that she was perfectly sincere about it. Why shouldn't he consult her? Men of great wealth often did, crediting their success to her intervention with My Lord Satan. Surely, she could do the same for Marc Meridon!

Damn him! He was not smiling, but he seemed to find her amusing, all the same.

"Not precisely. However, I want to thank you for your excellent work last night. You were very quick-witted."

"Oh—that! Well, there was nothing else to be done. The poor devil needed help. He seemed awfully anxious. And, as it turned out, he really was sicker than I thought." Before she finished speaking, she was aware that this was not what he was talking about, but his real meaning confused her only briefly. "You mean . . . Mrs. Deeth's son. I should have guessed."

"Yes. You should have guessed." Her reminded her with pleasant irony, "Your ability to communicate with the powers of darkness seems only to work in the service of others. Have you no wish to ask favors for yourself? You oblige so many people."

She laughed, although the trend of the conversation puzzled her. The only thing her perennially suspicious mind could come up with was that this might be his prelude to an attempt at buying her services, or getting control of the Coven business.

"Thank you. But I don't give these services for nothing, Mr. Meridon; so I can hardly take credit for altruism. I did suggest that Mrs. Deeth's boy might be benefitted here in the Cove, but that was only because—because—"

"You wanted to help me."

She certainly didn't want to confess she had been afraid of him in the brief time that he stared at her last night in the Mirror Bar. It had seemed to her at the time that he was communicating with her in that eerie mental fashion, reminding her to get on with the bit about curing Toby Deeth at Lucifer Cove. She had obliged. Maybe he did want to thank her. Upon reflection, she decided that she frankly deserved it. Let him offer his payment, if that was his intention.

She smiled modestly. "I suppose I did help you, in a sense. But I was thinking the boy might actually regain his health here. Did it work? I mean—" she corrected herself in a hurry, "is Mrs. Deeth going to have her son spend time with her here in the Valley?"

"She is making the arrangements now. We discussed the matter after you left us and Christine was a trifle recovered. You can appreciate her fears. There is so much debauchery in the world today and the contamination is everywhere."

Especially here! But she did not say this aloud.

"Anyone can appreciate her concern. Still," she looked up at him, her blue eyes fixed on his face in a disconcerting way, "I realize that you are often away from the Cove, attending to your many affairs..."

"Affairs of business."

Accentuating her innocence, she amended quickly, "Of course. But the point is, I should think you would like to have Mrs. Deeth with you occasionally on your journeys. To act as hostess; that sort of thing. And if her little boy is here, it might prove a handicap."

He said in a grim voice, "Very true. But I prefer to have him under my wing. That is to say, there may be things I can do for the child. I doubt if he is getting any better up there in the foggy city. And as it is vacation time, he won't be missing school."

"And he can always be back at his classes in September."

There was a tiny silence. "Yes," he agreed, as if his mind were far away on other matters. "That is true." He shrugged, as if throwing off a mood. "But this is not rewarding you for your help. The best payment I can make, I believe, is to advise you of an exceedingly attractive proposition."

Good Lord! A stock market tip! It was not precisely the kind of reward she had expected.

"Thank you. I am always interested in propositions, if they will improve the influence of the temple."

He smiled at the careful, pompous little remark. "Good. You had a spectacular success last evening, I understand."

She raised her head, astonished. "Spectacular failure, you mean! There was an accident. Or a practical joke. That infernal Dr. Haupt—what a sense of humor!—cut into my service, pretending to be Hitler. He scared everyone to death. They poured out and down the hill in an absolute tidal wave." A thought occurred to her. She added with a distinct edge to her voice, as a new suspicion flashed into her mind, "Or was that the whole idea?"

"I don't think I understand."

Undoubtedly, it had all been deliberately planned, and she said so. "Dr. Haupt deliberately caused that silly stampede in order to steal my customers—I mean My Lord Satan's followers! I suppose all those idiots fell right into place at Haupt's vile orgies."

"Not entirely, Miss Janos. Apparently, you are not aware of the latest developments." He put his hands on hers again and briefly shook them. She was impressed as always by the subtle power he exerted when he chose. Small wonder that a fastidious woman like Christine Deeth was enthralled by him in spite of her fear for her son's contamination. "I think I will let you discover your triumph for yourself. It will raise your spirits. Go out in the village now. See for yourself. I'll tell you nothing more. You will enjoy it better."

Bewildered, she watched him take his hands from hers, and smiling, wave toward the street beyond the pink walls of this room with its cocoon-like safety, its pretense that all its inhabitants were young, beautiful, unlined, unmarked either by the cruelties of life or by their own debauchery.

"And this is all you have to say to me, Sir? Just—go outside and walk up and down?"

"I leave the rest to you, Miss Janos. I have the utmost confidence in your business judgment, and I don't wish to overpersuade you. I say only this: rely upon your own self-interest. It will serve you well. And you have me behind you as a double ... protection."

She didn't get up or leave until he was gone and even the light echo of his steps had ceased. She was thinking over the entire interview. For some reason it hadn't quite made sense. Marc Meridon felt he owed her a favor after her intervention about Toby Deeth. He had started to do something for her and then left her to do her own favors. It just might be that he had read her real character through the dumb facade she put up for him. In that case, he knew exactly how she trusted only her own unpressured decisions.

She got up, feeling a trifle shaky and not sure why. She went out into the hall, passed a paunchy, sixtyish male newcomer to the Spa who was on his way to the blue-green pool with one of the Hot Springs girls. The man nudged his companion, whispered audibly, in some Middle-European accent. Nadine couldn't place: "Who is that? Her eyes terrify one. Not so?"

The blonde grinned over her shoulder at Nadine. She was the girl O'Flannery had hired as the Altar Girl last night and she said breezily, "That's Devil Lady. Better not cross her. They say she has an evil eye."

For some reason this did not amuse or flatter Nadine as it might have done at another time. She went out on the quiet, sunny street in a thoughtful mood. As usual, there was not much excitement between those Tudor fronts that peered down at her like eyes too heavily underscored with mascara. Nor did she immediately discover what Marc Meridon had been talking about when he sent her out to take the pulse of the Cove's clients. She started north toward the Hot Springs which looked subdued and harmless, baking in the hazy sunlight. The only reminders of that significant and horrifying black smoke this morning were the little spirals of sulphur snaking into the air from the grounds and the outdoor sulphur pool. Nadine had occasionally bathed in that pool but since awakening yesterday as a virtual prisoner of the Hot Springs tribe she no longer found that even the outside pool had any attraction for her.

Edna Schallert was walking along with stout little Mr. Buddy Hemplemeier who would obviously have preferred younger company. He kept eying two Hot Springs girls across the street. Seeing Nadine, Edna called, "It was devastating last night, Miss Janos. How ever did you do it? Mr. Hemplemeier says he's completely sold on you after that devil showed up." Buddy nodded vigorously, his mind on the girls across the street. "Keep up your good work," Edna added.

Nadine agreed to do so, not entirely sure what she had agreed to do. Partway up the street, she saw the gift shop and pharmacy run by the woman, Mrs. Peasecod, generally known in the Cove as "The Old Witch." The shop had an interesting bow window full of toys and gifts of various sorts, mostly toiletries. A woman she recognized only as one of the Coven passed behind Nadine as she looked at the display in the bow window. Nadine saw her face reflected in the glass and it was evident the woman thought of avoiding Nadine, then changed her mind.

"Marvelous show last night, Miss Janos. Simply incredible."

Wondering if this was a subtle form of sarcasm, Nadine said coldly, "Thank you. We do our best."

"Yes, and very well, too. But the truth is, I never really believed you could raise the devil. I mean—what a frightening power to have!"

"Oh. That!" What *was* she talking about?

The woman went on and Nadine, seeing O'Flannery's favorite after-shave, went in to get it and to see if Mrs. Peasecod had delivered the communion liquor containing its hint of drugs along with the other revolting contents. The Old Witch came shuffling out from some doubtless cob-webby regions behind the counter, dressed, as she often was, in a kind of Hawaiian holoku that she turned inside out when one side got too soiled. The ragged seams were all fully revealed, and though she appeared loathesome, she was exactly the sort of ancient hippie who might be expected to brew a devilish concoction of toads and snakes and any assorted earthworms not otherwise engaged.

"Ah, Girlie," she greeted Nadine familiarly in her toothy way. "It's a hit you've made, let me tell you. How did you ever think to have your trick devil pop up looking like Hitler instead of the old boy with the forked tail?"

"But I didn't! I mean—Doesn't everyone in the Cove see Dr. Haupt's resemblance to Hitler?"

The old woman's hard, watery eyes stared at her. "Not so's you'd notice. Or maybe a little mite around the cheekbones. But I'd have thought the mustache. . . . Well, the Führer, the way I remember him, has the silly Chaplin mustache, and this kraut's got a normal bit of hair, kind of ordinary."

Nadine shivered and then said with a forced smile. "I wish you wouldn't refer to Adolf Hitler in the present tense. Gives me the creeps."

"Them guys never die, so long's one person remembers them," Mrs. Peasecod leaned over the counter. "If I was to put the finger on one candidate for the devil in this place, I'd make it your friend Erich Haupt. He's one sharp cookie, and nasty as hell, for all his smiles and his nicey-nice behavior, like butter don't melt in his mouth. When that kind behaves like that they're generally lookin' for a better job. I had a counter woman acted same way one time. She wanted my job. How you like *them* apples?"

This amused Nadine and brought her miraculously out of the chilling depression that held her in its grip in recent hours. She bought the aftershave bottle and inquired about the next delivery of communion wine to the temple. When she left the shop the woman called after her, "Mind what I say now."

"I'll mind," Nadine promised. But she had suddenly made up her mind, influenced by the woman's own inverted praise of Erich Haupt. He was useful, he was clever, and he had clearly increased her business last night, though she hadn't suspected it at the time.

A few minutes later she stopped in at the Hot Springs Reception Office to ask Dr. Haupt if he cared to combine their efforts at the temple temporarily. She would keep an eye on him, see that he didn't overstep the boundaries she set for him, both personal and business, and he just might prove to be a big help, as so many people had gone out of their way to indicate this morning.

TEN

"Hey there, Miss J. Nice going last night at the Coven meet," some man called from the poolside within the big fence that enclosed the grounds of the Hot Springs.

Nadine didn't recognize the speaker, one of the bronze-bodied youngish characters surrounded by similar males and christened by the regular clientele of Lucifer Cove "The Gay Boys Sextette." Nadine's main objection to the Sextette was that it subtracted so many of those hard-to-find, good looking males from the situations where they were needed, among the oversupply of women. However, the whole object of the Cove, so far as Nadine could make out, was "Everybody do his own thing" until surfeited of it.

And then? Many ways to quit, most of them both unpleasant and permanent. There were some who left the Cove and returned to prosaic lives outside. But to accomplish this, they seemed, according to Nadine's interested study, people who threw off the temptations which permeated the Cove. Not easy. Not easy, at all; for it meant that they had to stop using the byword of Lucifer Cove:

"I'll do, or enjoy, or whatever . . . once more today, for the last time. And I'll break off tomorrow."

But tomorrow always turned up as just another "today."

I must remember that, Nadine told herself firmly as she followed the bright border of marigolds, leading her to the Reception Door of the Hot Spring. I've got to remember to quit before I let this place get to be my whole life.

Since all passages at the Springs were indicated by colors, she was amused at the "gold" symbolism of the marigolds. It was the sort of thing that would bring tears to the eyes of sentimental drunks. Of course, she liked the marigolds herself. But her reasons were not dictated by sentiment or alcohol. She liked the marigolds because they were bright, cheerful, and their gold represented prosperity to her.

"I'm different from the others at the Cove. They are all rushing downhill. I am rapidly climbing up."

It was odd, the tricks her mind played. She had found it remarkably difficult to make her way out through the intricacies of the Hot Springs. But it was the simplest thing in the world to work her way into the heart of the place. In spite of this fact, she was careful to note every twist and turn in the halls, every different color indicating offshoots into areas she would as soon not investigate. They didn't mean any profit for her, and she was far from interested in joining Erich Haupt in his enterprise, at any rate.

One of the powerful amazonian beauties Dr. Haupt seemed to prefer in authority around the place was on duty behind the Reception Desk. She greeted Nadine with an effusiveness out of all proportion to Nadine's presumed importance to her.

"My dear Miss Janos! Do come . . . that is, sit down. Let me find—" she got on the intercom. "Isabel, leave those others and come in a minute. I need you." To Nadine she explained, "I'm going to send for one of the masseurs. Typical tiresome males, my dear, but what can you expect? However—there is a new masseuse who is marvelous. Would you prefer—?" She was pressing the buzzer and snapping the intercom again. "Maia, come in, please." She looked at Nadine. "They'll turn you inside out and make you a fresh girl."

"I can imagine!" Nadine told herself silently and corrected the woman aloud, "No, thank you. I wanted to see Dr. Haupt, on business, if I may." She added quickly. "Tell him it's about business. Remember."

Slightly flustered, the young woman repeated, "About business? We understand. The only difficulty—that is, he isn't in right now. He's away. Something came up suddenly. We're having trouble with some new deliveries and the Doctor finally had to supervise them himself. We're being held up on price and some minor difficulties, and if you know Doctor, you know he's not one to hold still for that."

Though Nadine agreed indifferently, with a fine pretense of boredom at these ramblings, she had early learned to pigeonhole all gratuitous information for the future. She never knew when, in her business, there might be a chance to use information that the client did not know she knew. It was precisely this sort of thing that made horrified and very much impressed clients accuse her of witchcraft. While she stood there smiling vaguely, as if about to turn away and leave, she let the girl's information file itself neatly in her brain, asking herself at the same time what deliveries Haupt had to dash out and rescue? Beautiful creatures, probably, of both sexes. And who was holding up Haupt for these Hot Springs Delights? Procurers of one sort or another.

The whole business did not immediately sound like anything useful to her. She raised her head, about to give up and go when she became aware of a blast of air-conditioning that hit her hard between the shoulders. She looked around, saw that a door had opened and one of the Hot Springs girls, pert in a spectacular pink micro-mini outfit that looked transparent but was only opaque.

"Don't be only half-safe," Nadine remarked but the girl didn't get it. She was looking anxiously at the Receptionist.

"Are they back? My boyfriend called me before six. Said they'd had difficulties with the ghouls who—"

"Maia!" called the Receptionist sternly.

The girl colored, glanced at Nadine, noticing her for the first time. "I thought she knew everything."

"Maia," the Receptionist cut in with great clarity. "Is one of the masseurs free? We'd like Miss Janos to meet them. If we knew your tastes, Miss Janos, we could direct you properly."

"My tastes are mainly . . ." What did one say in a case like that? If she said her tastes were normal, they would not necessarily be normal to these overstuffed lovelies. Nadine was not too interested in masseurs of masseuses, especially at this hour, but she became more and more interested in these little snippets of conversation which were dropping around her. She pretended to reconsider, turning, looking the girl Maia up and down, beginning an expression as lascivious and erotic as she could work up at short notice. It was not the easiest thing she had ever done, because the women obviously supposed they attracted her, whereas, the girl Maia's fleshy temptation suggested to Nadine nothing so much as a burlesque dancer, with the Receptionist as an over-exerting gym teacher.

"Your tastes, you were saying, Miss Janos?" the Receptionist prompted her with a grim smile and a nod at Maia behind her.

Nadine looked suitably embarrassed. "Perhaps you might show me around your lovely quarters today. Only that. A little tour. Then I can return another time."

"Another . . . night?" suggested the Receptionist politely, but giving Maia such a nasty smirk Nadine felt strongly inclined to slap off the smirk. Did they really think they could win her as if she were an ordinary hedonist, ready to be tempted into her own destruction?

"Er . . . yes. Some night. I haven't much time, Maia. Shall we go?"

The sexy Maia took her by the arm.

A lamb to the slaughter, Nadine thought, wondering how she would get the girl off her sex kick and back onto the ghouls, and Dr. Haupt's mysterious journey. It just might mean a great deal to Nadine if she could discover what he was up to.

"Be nice to the lady now, Maia," the Receptionist's voice pursued them down a corridor, and Maia's handclasped Nadine's arm more tightly, reminding Nadine that she was no match for these amazons. She said in a bright, idiot way.

"I just adore the perfume in these halls. Notice it?"

"Oh, yes, Miss Janos. This is the lilac passage. The scent is piped into this area with the air-conditioning."

Nadine sniffed. Her personal preference was for a modern, sophisticated scent, and this one was wildly erotic, with what seemed to be tons of patchouli. It suggested nothing to Nadine as much as an overstuffed harem.

Maia twitched a little. "Like it? Don't it make you feel good? I could just climb walls when I smell it." She did an explicit grind.

They were moving through an exercise room, or what purported to be one. Nadine had her suspicions about the use of phallic symbols for the varied objects that women were working on. The slant boards, the too-cozy twist belt, the "horse"—more like a centaur, an absurd unicorn whose symbolism and use were even more obvious, and the musclebound male who was presiding over these globular females.

Before Maia could get carried away by the wonder of it all, Nadine murmured, "I can't seem to get the proper charge out of it, as long as my boyfriend is out there fussing around with those . . . ghouls."

"What?" This put a different look on things.

Maia's eyes evidenced. "You got a man? I mean, I thought you were one of them. You know. Double-gaited."

"Never mind that." Damn! Wouldn't the girl ever back onto important matters? "Do you think there will be any trouble about the ghouls?" She had almost nothing to go on and felt with every word that she was liable to betray her ignorance of the affair. But there was something important behind these hints, something that could possibly mean money to the temple, which had been her first thought. Other motives prompted her curiosity now. Dr. Haupt and his unsavory group were up to some messy business. If it proved to be too unpleasant, Marc Meridon might be interested. If he did have a financial part in this hole, he wouldn't want to see it ruined by some wild stuff introduced into the Hot Springs by Erich Haupt.

"Of course, it might all be some silly game they're playing," she said thinking out loud.

"Sure you don't want to go in and try out the Exercise Room, Miss Janos?"

Nadine looked into the room, got a beckoning finger from a fat lady mounting the unicorn, and turned away hurriedly. "Thanks but no thanks. I'm so worried about my boyfriend. When do you think they'll get back. And do you think they'll be successful?" That stab in the dark was as close as she dared to get without revealing her own ignorance.

Maia released her arm so suddenly, Nadine cracked her elbow against the lilac wall. Rubbing it with brisk, hard movements, she watched the girl. She began to hope she was finally go-

150

ing to get some clue. The girl looked around, giggling nervously.

"Well, yes. After all, it's worked so far; hasn't it? Kind of gives me the creeps, but then, I always did have kooky tastes. I'm really with it. I get frizzy thinking about it. Don't you?"

"In a way. That is, sometimes I think so." She breathed quickly, liking the sound of Dr. Haupt's scheme less and less.

After that, Maia reached over Nadine's head, pushing a door open and while her arm was in that position, she looked down at Nadine. A direct, unblinking look that filled Nadine with a revulsion which affected her like a violent stomach upheaval.

"You know, Miss Janos, you got groovy eyes. You'd go over big here. The Doc says you and he might go into business together." She shifted her arm. There was a faint rime of sweat on her upper lip.

Furthermore, that upper lip could use a shave Nadine thought unkindly. She ducked under the girl's arm, but at the same time, the door fell open under the girl's pressure and Nadine found herself tumbling into a dimly lighted room, heavy with some Oriental scent or other, and featuring, as she saw at once, a husky, blonde woman and a lilac covered plinth. The blonde "masseuse" was grinning at her. The grin had the effect of that earlier beckoning finger.

The whole thing was so utterly ridiculous, she wondered even then why she was so terrified. What could the woman do to her? But it was always the same fear, that she would find herself in the power of someone else. Physical or mental or emotional dominance, it was all the same. She dreaded the thought of someone else manipulating her life for her.

The big, good looking, hideous woman began to stride toward her on bouncy shoe soles. "Come in, Miss. You're welcome, you know. I'll show you around. We have a darling section here with little knick-knacks from the women's wards of certain camps some years ago in—well, in Eastern Europe. Interested, dearies?"

What enormous hands the woman had! All thumbs, thick pink muscles reaching out to her.

Nadine scratched out wildly at Maia's restraining hands, and while the two women collided into each other with suitable grunts, she dashed out and down the hall. She heard something behind her very like laughter, and was not too surprised. But still she ran. She was anxious to avoid that Exercise Room and had to take a corridor on her left just before reaching the big, obscene room itself. The red line marking the way seemed oddly familiar and she realized she must have crossed this corridor the morning Meridon and Irish got her out of the Clinic. The symbolism of the red color was not lost on her, and she hurriedly crossed into the next corridor that branched off, again on her left.

She was scurrying along in her mindless panic, expecting momentarily to wind up in the Reception Room when she discovered that the corridor was marked in black. This was even worse. Death. With all the symbolism here, black certainly indicated death. She very nearly turned back to take her chances with Maia and friends. As it was, she thought she heard the echo of those bouncing shoes worn by the muscular masseuse and told herself this labyrinth simply had to end somewhere near the out-of-doors.

Ahead, the indirect neon lighting that bordered the ceiling became suddenly brighter. An eerie, depressing blue light was cast across the hall floor from a partially open door, still on Nadine's left. She stopped, moved quietly along until she could see around the heavy door and into the blue-lighted room which was a laboratory, equipped in a sterile but probably utilitarian way, and presided over by two men emptying various receptacles of different sizes and shapes. They reminded her of workers from a sanitation department except that they wore black cobbler's aprons over white lab technician uniforms. She thought the obvious explanation was that the slops and debris of the clinic were disposed of here. Another room beyond opened out of the laboratory and by squinting and peering intently at that room, she was able to make out a huge brickwork affair at the far center.

Suddenly one of the men took a barrel of debris, swung it onto his shoulder and carried it to the brickwork where he raised his foot and shoved open the door in the center. She should have guessed it was an incinerator. With the door open, the flames like greedy tongues reached out at the worker who tossed his whole load in, barrel and all. To Nadine, the real shocker was the size of the incinerator door. Large enough to engulf any conceivable object that men would find portable.

It had taken Nadine rather longer than she considered necessary for a woman of intelligence to discover that, in all likelihood, those persons who died at the Clinic and left no family to claim their remains, were cremated here with the rest of the unwanted and used-up trash.

Ashes to ashes, she thought, and shuddered. She had never believed she would pity Ricardo Shahnaz.

Suddenly, without any forewarning, the other handler raised his head. His eyes, deep-socketed and shadowy in his pale face, seemed to pick out Nadine, and stare at her unblinking. She didn't dare move. Surely, he couldn't make out her features. The light in the sterile white laboratory was brighter than the indirect hall lighting. But, more and more curious, he made no sign that he had seen her at all. After several endless seconds, he looked away. She wondered if he could be blind. At any rate, this was not a place she care to hang around any longer than necessary. She moved rapidly past the door, cursed the bit of sand on the stone floor that made a gritty sound, and was grateful when the hall turned at a sharp angle and magically widened, with three corridors emptying into it. None of the familiar color indications were there. Neither orange nor blue struck a sympathetic cord, but green certainly ought to lead to the blessed out-of-doors.

It was a long hall but the walls were of a soft, pale green, the lighting imitated sunlight, and there was about it the haunting smell of spring grass. She slowed to a walk, listened and heard the distant drone of a plane somewhere overhead. Civilization, of sorts, was still around.

When she came out into the actual sunlight she found herself in a glass-enclosed cloister with a brickwork floor and a charming little patio whose central fountain made a pleasant suggestion of coolness during the mid-day heat. No one was out here now. Too hot, probably. Or was it deserted, after all? No. Someone sat huddled there on the far side of the fountain. A man in his fifties or slightly older, lean and suffering, his straight, thinning gray hair plastered against his skull by the splashing water from the fountain. A man distinguished in some intellectual field, Nadine thought. When he heard her step on the gravel, he looked around vaguely. She recognized him as the agonized man she had passed on the south bridge the night before.

"Ah," he said without enthusiasm. "It is you, Miss Janos." His smile was thin and an obvious effort. Like his blood, it was watery, she thought with a faint contempt. She did not find his homosexual tastes so contemptible as his hopelessness, his lack of spirit. Once an internationally famous violinist, he let a silly 'love affair' get him down.

"Good afternoon, Mr. Illich. Isn't it a bit warm out here? You'd be more comfortable in the baths."

He shook his head. "No. I cannot. He is there. My friend. We—we quarrelled. I do not wish to embarrass him."

"Forgive me, but if that is so, you are free to return to your career; aren't you? Your talent

155

has been very much missed, you know. I was reading only last week in San Francisco how the Zurich and Vienna Symphonies have missed you. And the Berlin..."

She saw she wasn't getting through to him. The silly fool thought more of his broken love affair than his fabulous ability, his international fame. "My career. What is that? A cold, inhuman thing. We were so... so suited."

She made an altogether false sound of sympathy and was figuring out how to get out of this Hot Springs torture hole, when he bestirred himself enough to reach out and catch at her sleeve.

"Miss Janos! You have powers."

"I am said to have powers. Yes." Called to remember her own reputation as a seer, an unearthy contact with the powers of darkness, she stiffened a little, squared her shoulders and turned into the devil's priestess. Sergi Illich was too concerned with his own unhappiness to be surprised at her transition.

"Just so, Miss Janos. Then is it not possible for some special prayer to be said... I can made it well worth your while."

"Please, Mr. Illich! No *my* while. You may give what you feel your prayer is worth, but let it be understood that your gift is devoted to what we may call *better relations with My Lord Satan*."

Somewhat confused, he nodded, watching her now with a wisp of hope in his anguished eyes. "I shall attend your next seance." He saw her reaction, corrected himself hastily. "Your Coven Meeting, I believe you call it."

"Very well, Mr. Illich. And we shall see if My Lord Satan will oblige you. We promise nothing. But we may hope."

She thanked him, feeling pleasantly enthused over his praise in spite of herself, and decided to be honest about her own problem.

"How the devil—" She caught herself before she lowered her own priestly status. "How the devil's name do you get out of this labyrinth?"

"Oh, that! Of course. Just beyond the wall at that east corner."

"What? I don't see how." But when she crossed the patio, she saw that the intricate brickwork wall was actually double, and that by the time she reached it, there were a narrow passage behind and parallel to the wall. She took this passage, and within a few yards was out in a thicket of heath and dry plants that crept over what was virtually a series of vacant lots behind the Tudor buildings that faced the Cove's main street.

She stood a few minutes breathing deeply what she thought of as free air, but her nose reminded her at once of the sulphur beneath the surface of this dry, cracked ground. She still had to cross these fields and make her way back onto the street. Since there seemed no shorter route, the obvious route was through or between those stark black and white Tudor buildings.

"Now is my chance to satisfy that old urge," she decided.

She had always been curious about those buildings which looked too pristine, and fresh-painted, too "pretty" to be properly lived in like the Spa and the Hot Springs where the nervous gaiety, and the despair appeared to seep out of the walls themselves. Today she had the ideal excuse to cover any charge of trespassing if she was found behind those picturesque little Tudor windows.

And Lucifer Cove was one place where she preferred not to be caught trespassing, in any direction!

It was a hot, unpleasant hike through briars, thistle and over assorted spirals of sulphurous smoke, and she was glad to reach a rear door along the first block of houses. No one answered her knock and she stood on her toes and peered in the window of what she supposed must be a kitchen or a utility room. She was surprised to find it empty and even more surprised, upon closer examination, to discover that the room was only half constructed.

Pressing her nose against the window which smelled of heat and the dry, parched wood frame, she could see the unfinished beams, the hall with no floor, merely boards laid over sand and gravel, and beyond that, the carefully constructed Tudor windows with small, opaque panes.

"And they call me a phony!"

Still, this might possibly be the only false front along the stretch of several blocks. She moved along, now thoroughly curious, and found the same sham buildings, everywhere. When nothing more interesting turned up, she tried the doors repeatedly, and finally found one whose lock was jammed. It seemed odd that the door had been locked at all. There was nothing in these playhouses that looked to be of value.

Nadine gave up the unrewarding detective act and pushing hard, releasing the catch on the door. With any luck, she could unlatch one of those false Tudor front doors and find herself in the main street of Lucifer Cove. The interior of the fake house was not quite dark, due to the light filtered through the small glass panes, but it was still easy to trip over half-finished flooring, and to be confused by stairs leading upward into nothingness.

Walking through shadows to avoid the hard pebble floor, she paid the penalty of falling from one danger into another and was tripped up by a pitcher or ceramic pot. She fell over it, and less pained than angry at her own clumsiness, stared at the pot while feeling for tears and rips in her pleated pajama legs.

Of all the odd quirks, the pot was sealed. Like something out of the Arabian Nights. She felt the pot, held it nearer but couldn't make it out too clearly. Whatever precious ointment, or weird souvenir the pot contained, some other Sinbad would have to open it. She got to her feet, thankful that she hadn't broken an ankle, and with her first step heard a crunch underfoot.

She reached down, wondering what she had gotten into, and picked up a small metal rectangle engraved with a name and number. There were soldered bits on the back of the metal. It had evidently broken off from something. She held it up to the window light and read a name:

GAYLIE MERRILL
2307

What the devil! The only Gaylie Merrill she had ever heard of was the sexy raven-haired film star who had cut her wrists and then drowned in her estate pool a year before.

Tapping the little piece of silver against her thumb nail, she tried to figure out where she had seen this sort of engraved metal piece before. The answer hit her along with a ghastly chill. Nadine's mother had been cremated. The ashes were in an urn and the name and number on the mausoleum wall were very like this. In a kind of emotional slow motion Nadine looked down at the "ceramic vase" she had stumbled over. Or was it, in fact, a sealed urn?

ELEVEN

It was the wrong minute to hear an alien sound. A pebble turned over somewhere in the shadows. She didn't call out but waited, holding her breath. There was a slight scuffling sound. She exhaled impatiently.

"Kinkajou! Is that you?"

The little striped tabby cat obligingly scuttled over to nuzzle her ankles.

"How did you get in here? Were you locked in?"

He meowed piteously, as he always did whenever he hadn't been fed. How long had he been trapped in here? She questioned him again and got only a wide open mouth full of feline teeth, followed by another complaint.

Now, if Kinkajou's tongue were only as eloquent as his big, gray-green eyes, he could tell her who had stored the urn in here and incidentally who had, inadvertently, no doubt, locked the cat in. She looked around squinting into the dark sectors of the room. The place appeared to be empty except for a pile of boards stacked on the gravel-strewn dirt floor. She had a horrid thought suddenly, and stepped back to run her fingers over the boards, but they appeared innocent enough. No disinterred coffins, which were what she half expected to discover.

Kinkajou slinked along after her, a nerve wracking presence in the dark. She reached down, picked up the cat and found his body warm and comforting, against her breast. Strange how temperamental he was! A day or so ago he had been scratching and spitting freely. Even with his claws, or maybe because of his claws, he seemed extraordinarily human.

"What's going on in here, Kinky?"

He didn't bother to deal with her question. He put a paw up and gently reminded her that she hadn't settled his more urgent problem. She shook off the horror that made her rush around rubbing boards, and concentrated on getting out. What appeared to be the street door turned out to be nailed shut. She gave up after a few minutes and retraced her steps, stopping at what ought to have been a kitchen. This time she saw a door in the south wall and forced it open. It was only stuck. She found herself in a similar half-built Hollywood prop set. Nothing at all, except where it could be seen by anyone peeking in through one of those murky little window panes. From that vantage point on the front sidewalk there were bits and pieces that suggested someone lived here.

She found no more urns, nor any coffins, although she was suspicious enough to look.

A short while later, with prodding from Kinkajou, she gave up, tried the makeshift front door and this time it worked. The door was bolted from the inside. Once she shot the bolt, and clenched her teeth at the grating noise of the door opening, she was out on the Cove's main street with Kinkajou, and glad to be there.

It was too hot for many of the Cove's sybaritic residents to be on the street, but she did see the girl, Araby, stifling a yawn, come out of the Spa up the street and after a moment's indecision, turn and go up toward the Hot Springs. In spite of her jealousy, Nadine was not blind to the girl's attractions, her graceful, leggy stride, the gorgeous, thick auburn hair worn to her shoulders, a softening halo for the Garboesque contours of her face.

"I don't doubt she's just come from O'Flannery."

At the same time she knew that by treating Irish so badly, she had left him wide open to the efforts of a sexpot like Araby What's-Her-Name. What nobody in the world understood was that if she gave herself over wholly to Irish or any other human being—not just her body but her full devotion, she would lose him much more quickly. Always dangle the extra emotion out of reach.

Anyway, she thought with a wry smile, it's worked so far!

She had very little confidence in the ability of a loving, giving, masochistic Navidia Janocek to hold a man. Life was two short to waste in experiments.

Kinkajou squirmed nervously in her arms. She looked down at him, caressing the soft fur. His nervousness was contagious. But she had seen and heard nothing unusual since leaving the Tudor false fronts. The contents of that one room were quite enough to satisfy Nadine's taste for the outré, the strange. The explanation that she suspected still filled her with dread. The more she thought of it, the more she hoped someone like Marc Meridon could clear up the mystery with a casual explanation that would satisfy her. She was prepared to be easily satisfied.

The cat squirmed and her fingers automatically tightened their hold on him. Out came the claws and Nadine quickly released him, sucking her scratched knuckles and glaring at him angrily.

"Get along! Go on! Scat!"

Kinkajou darted away, across the sidewalk to the covered passage beside the Spa, which led to the parking lot behind the big building. Along the pebbled ground of the passageway Nadine heard footsteps. It was here that Kinkajou stopped abruptly. She followed him, tense and irritated at herself for being so easily frightened.

"Hello, Kittycat. Here, Kittycat," called a small, high-pitched childish voice and as Nadine reached the passage she saw what undoubtedly was Christine Deeth's boy, Toby. He was a plain, pale, freckled-faced little fellow with his mother's beautiful smile but nothing else impressive about him except his heavy limp and the way he ignored the limp. He was reaching out for the cat who studied him with unblinking interest but did not make any advances toward him. When the boy saw Nadine, he looked up with a shy grin.

"Hello. I'm Toby Deeth."

Nadine took the sturdy young hand he offered.

"Welcome to Lucifer Cove, Toby Deeth. I am Nadine Janos."

"That's pretty . . . Nadine. What do you do?"

She felt a surprising and entirely unaccustomed embarrassment. "I am a priestess."

"Priestess? I know about priests. I didn't know they had priestesses."

Christie's voice called from the parking lot beyond the passage. "Toby? Toby dear, where are you?"

Toby slipped his hand out of Nadine's with a polite, "Excuse me. My mother wants me . . . I'm here, Mom! I met a cat. And a lady priest."

Christie Deeth appeared at the end of the passage, hurrying toward the boy who limped to her. Nadine watched them, unaccountably moved by the sight of the two and their obvious devotion. She waved to Christine who smiled back at her over Toby's sandy head and after a moment, noticeable to Nadine, she returned the wave.

I'm still poison to that dame, Nadine reminded herself. She couldn't figure it out. She had her job to do, like anybody else. What gave Christie Deeth, Adulteress, the superiority complex? Nevertheless, she was grateful to the woman for her reminder of Nadine's position.

I'm Nadine Janos. I'm the Devil's Priestess. Get out of my way, world.

She strolled through the passageway, remembering to square her shoulders and walk tall. It was hellish to be short and to be forced to cultivate a tall image as she had done all her life.

"Mrs. Deeth, I wonder if you could help me."

Christine looked at her, really trying to be

165

friendly. The trouble was, Nadine was sure she saw the effort it cost her.

"Anything I can do to help you, Miss Janos. I seem to recall I asked you the same question last night; didn't I?" She ruffled up Toby's hair and the boy squirmed like Kinkajou, muttering with a little giggle and a sneeze.

"You tickle, Mom."

"And now, my boy is here, and I hope none of us will be sorry."

Startled at this frankness in the boy's presence, Nadine said hurriedly, "I'm sure none of us will be, Mrs. Deeth. We'll all look after him. We just won't let any—any evil come to him. I swear it."

"You have some specific evil in mind?" Mrs. Deeth smiled bleakly. They were walking along together to the front of the Spa. Toby had reached for Kinkajou, but the cat, having satisfied his curiosity about the boy, turned and slipped away into the darkness at the back of the passage.

"Never mind, Toby," his mother consoled him. "There will be other animals eventually. Dogs, maybe. We'll have Mr. Meridon find you a dog. You'd like that; wouldn't you?" She looked at Nadine. "He's allergic to cats. They make him sneeze. He can't stand being too close to them."

"Yes. Speaking of Mr. Meridon, I'd like to see him. I have a problem. Something I saw a little while ago that I think he should know about."

Christine frowned. Nadine had a notion she had missed something. The woman was acting very oddly. "But he isn't in the Cove. You know he never stays here very long at a time. He has so many interests everywhere."

"Oh." Nadine was stuck. "I wonder who else I could see."

"Why not try Dr. Haupt? He seems to handling the Hot Springs with a great deal of finesse. Excuse me. This is where Toby and I leave you, I'm afraid."

Nadine was left on the sidewalk with a violent feeling that her face had been slapped. To be offered Dr. Haupt as her adviser on the ghoulish habit of stealing the ashes of dead film stars, was riotously funny, if Christine Deeth only knew it. Or did she?

Nadine shivered.

A few minutes later, from a phone in the pink salon, she called up to her suite in the Spa and got no answer. Heaven knew where Irish was! She decided to go back to her dubious haven on the hillside. There were times when she felt at home only in her temple, in spite of recent odd happenings there.

Cheerless and prey to all kinds of forebodings, she restored to her own healing method which had worked for her all her life. She walked rapidly, head up, taking as many deep breaths as she could, handicapped in the latter by a heavy, constricting weight on her chest. The weight of fear.

What have I gotten into? What is this place? I've done so well here, must I run away from my success? Fate? Power of Darkness? Whoever or whatever rules our lives, I'll make you a bargain. Give me one more successful month. Two at the outside. I'll save the profits. Invest them, and

Irish and I will leave here and start up somewhere else...

Los Angeles was a good place for a killing. There were a lot of nuts down there who ate up cults, devil and otherwise. *But Los Angeles was where the urn of Gaylie Merrill's ashes came from.*

"Yes, and God knows how many more grave robberies. Is this what Irish was talking about this morning? Is Haupt mixed up in it? I wish Meridon was here. He'd know what to do, how to advise me. . . . I could go outside the Cove and report this business to the county authorities. . . .

But some self-protective voice inside her warned her that this would be fatal, and she didn't know precisely why. It was not the ordinary fear of reprisal. It was beyond that and took her several minutes to confess the truth to herself: she was not entirely sure of Marc Meridon. There were times when he baffled and worried her in spite of his attractions. Maybe because of them. She, who almost always got a person's number, found the weakness, learned how best to outwit that person, had never satisfactorily solved the riddle of Marc Meridon.

She had nearly reached the bridge over the dry creek, relieved at the lengthening shadows of sunset that promised some relief from the heat when she passed Edna Schallert coming down from her chalet. She still seemed in those good spirits which she had earlier that day shown in stout little Buddy Hemplemeier's company.

"Hello, Miss Janos. I must thank you again for

that frightfully intriguing service last night. I can't tell you how you lifted my spirits. One of your prayers to My Lord Satan was definitely about me; wasn't it? And your psychic guide—of all people, to conjure up the man Satan would most likely listen to, that horrid Adolf Hitler! Anyway, I've sold some of those securities I promised you, and the proceeds are in your name, for your—" She tittered and covered her mouth briefly, "—your Big Boss. Well, 'bye now. I'm off to meet Buddy at the Hot Springs."

Edna Schallert at the Hot Springs! What next? Nadine was careful not to laugh. She had just started across the bridge, rapidly increasing her distance from Edna who was going in the opposite direction, when Edna exclaimed sharply, in what was a virtual panic.

"Scat! Go 'way! Don't touch me, you hear? Scat!"

It had to be Kinkajou.

Nadine looked over her shoulder. Sure enough, the little tabby cat was stalking toward Edna Schallert with that malicious sense of humor that Nadine had always observed and enjoyed in felines who seemed to delight in hanging around people they terrified. Edna was so clearly in difficulties, unable to move a step while the cat was in her path that Nadine took pity on her.

"Kinkajou! Come along."

Slightly to her surprise, he obeyed, leaving Edna Schallert to hurry on toward her tryst with the fat little Texan while he stalked Nadine. The latter looked down at him and laughed.

"Don't think you'll scare me, you little rascal! I know your tricks. You and I are alike, Boy, so you can stop that put-on, pretending you're a tiger. Stripes don't make the cat, Kinky!"

She could have sworn he grinned up at her, showing his needle-sharp teeth in a pink mouth. He did have his odd moments, but then, so did she. And she meant it when she accused him of being like her. All that effort of his to look mysterious. He might fool others, but under all the hypnotic eyes and graceful slinking ways, he was, like Nadine bereft of her careful poise, her chosen wardrobe, and her particularly effective use of her unusual eyes, just another cat at heart!

She crossed the bridge, thinking about cats she had owned—or who had owned her—and about the past, the dreaming, scheming past of her youth. Her fingers tingled as if the circulation had been cut off. She stumbled slightly as her foot began to show similar symptoms. She was not at the moment attuned to the present time and had not once thought of that sad old fellow, Sergei Illich, since she left him in the Hot Springs patio, and yet, when she stopped to stamp circulation back into her foot, as casually as she had seen Kinkajou a minute or two before, she now saw Sergi Illich lying low on the bank of the dry creek bed, in an almost fetal twist.

Nadine leaned over and stared at him from the flat board bridge. Among the gray pebbles of the creek bed, something glistened. The barrel of a hand gun of some kind, a European make and unfamiliar to her. But was he dead?"

"Mr. Illich!"

Kinkajou came over beside her and looked

down with a concentration that rivalled her own. Then he tilted his head and stared at her. Something in his persistent stare drew her attention.

"What is it now, you silly cat?"

Quite naturally, he had nothing to say to this, and she returned her attention to the bottom of the river bed and the apparent suicide of the unfortunate violinist. She blinked, opened, closed and opened her eyes rapidly. The crumpled body of the violinist was gone. So was the gun, or whatever the weapon had been.

She felt faint, her hands and feet prickling painfully as the blood returned to them and the numbness crept away. She carefully avoided the creek bed for a minute, studying the sunset beyond the distant sentinel rocks that guarded Lucifer Cove from the Coast Highway. The rocky barrier plunged the whole west end of the valley in deep shadow at this hour and lengthened all the other shadows so that even Kinkajou had his own weird and unnatural silhouette that extended over the bridge to the creek bed below.

Nadine tried to cultivate that enormous self-confidence which had so often got her out of difficulties, but it was hard going now She was absolutely convinced that she had seen Illich's body lying there; yet, common sense pointed to the obvious conclusion. A trick of light and shadow, the sometimes eerie effect of sunset had joined to produce the illusion.

"Either that or I've developed a talent that could be both useful and profitable. What do you think, Kinky? Am I losing my grip?"

Kinkajou put his head over the side plank of the bridge and peered down.

"See anything, Kinkajou?"

For answer, he pulled back his head and after a brief up and down glance at her, he stalked off the bridge.

"You're right," she agreed, following him. "I really must be uptight. Seeing dead bodies, imagining God knows what all. Wait for me, Kinky."

But all the way up the trail she was haunted by that strange brief vision she had experienced. All imagination? what, then, stimulated the thought which had seemed so real? Easy enough to dismiss it as the personification of some subconscious worry, but Nadine knew herself well. She didn't waste time worrying over weak-willed, hopeless cases like that of Sergei Illich. Her self-centered nature also allowed her to be honest about herself, and the whole explanation that she saw visions because of her concern for someone else was totally false to that Navidia Janocek she knew so well.

No other explanation occurred to her during that day, although she had new qualms about her own recent life when she went through the main auditorium of the temple and gazed up at the altar. It had begun here, above the altar, strangeness, an eerie sense that the Unnatural had intruded on her superbly self-ordered life.

No doubt, Kinkajou saw work ahead and no time for catnip. He went his way and Nadine found herself completely alone, a situation growing increasingly less attractive these days. And nights.

She spent a busy time reorganizing the props

for the next ceremony and was in the midst of this when she heard a confusion of voices outside and then footsteps in the portico. She was disgusted with herself when she found out how relieved she was at the intrusion. Hurriedly shutting the curtains behind which My Lord Satan obligingly appeared upon her request, she went up the nave aisle to the entry and saw O'Flannery's tall figure crossing between the pillars of the portico toward her and carrying a large, shadowy load draped across his arms.

"Visitors for you. Out of the way, Princess," he announced pleasantly. And he wasn't drunk. She was enormously relieved at that.

Puzzled over his remark about visitors, she made out the "bundle" in O'Flannery's arms, Young Toby Deeth's friendly eyes looked out at her from his tired, drawn face, and he said in a husky whisper, "Hi!"

She grinned at him, touched in spite of herself. "Hi, there. Had a little disaster, Fella?"

"Little one," he repeated after her, making a good effort to return her grin.

She frowned into the mauve dusk that shrouded the high world above the valley. "Irish, you said visitors?" But of course, the other visitor was Toby's mother, Christine Deeth. The woman came up the steps behind Irish, anxious and fatigued, starting to apologize for their intrusion.

"My son wanted so much to take a little hike, and his San Francisco doctors said it would be good for him. But I'm afraid we walked too far. I tried to carry Toby, but—"

"But I showed up on my way to the temple,"

Irish put in. "And made myself useful for a change. Nice to think I'm good for something."

Nadine didn't know whether this was a reminder to her, but as she snapped on the lights and led the way inside, Mrs. Deeth seconded him with great feeling.

"And you certainly came to our rescue, Mr. O"Flannery. We can't thank you enough. Miss Janos, I hope we aren't in your way. We will only stay long enough to get our breath. Toby is perfectly all right, you understand. Just tired out, poor lamb."

Nadine was oddly pleased to be responsible for her guests. She felt quite neighborly and middle-class. She assured Christie that they were welcome to stay and suggested to Irish, "We've got some Heublein cocktail bottles and some cans in the fridge back of the altarpiece; haven't we? And can't we get something for the boy to drink?"

"Some of your *communion wine?*" Irish asked her cuttingly, though he smiled when he said it.

"Oh, shut up! Come this way, Mrs. Deeth."

"You are very kind, but we'll try not to be a nuisance."

"Don't give it a thought." Nevertheless Nadine hated over-protestations. Remarks like this struck her as mealymouthed hyprocrisy. The woman had never liked her. Toby Deeth, on the other hand, had the makings of a thoroughly decent chap. Irish surprised Nadine by locating a cold can of root beer for the boy and while he and the women sat around on some of Nadine's props, Irish ran through the liquor menu:

"Can of Daiquiri. Bottle of-label's off. And a bottle of Margarita."

Christine ventured after a little hesitation, "I think maybe a drink of your communion wine would probably suit me as well as anything."

Irish was briefly speechless, but Nadine was so startled she burst into abrupt laughter that only made things worse between her and Christine, because the latter assumed she was being ridiculed. Irish explained hurriedly.

"It's a combination. Kind of Irish Stew of wines and whatnot, a wee dram of a drug in it, for calming effect, and something for . . ." He stopped. "Well, never mind that. Anyway, you wouldn't fancy it, Mrs. Deeth. Here. How's for a can of Vodka Martini? Better than a kick in the head."

Finally, they all found their tipple, Irish being forced to resort to the sweet Daiquiri with many a groan and a funny face that convulsed young Toby. They were still at their makeshift cocktails when Christine Deeth raised her head, listening intently. O'Flannery had been in the middle of an Irish dialect story and Nadine, admiring the personality he exerted when he chose to, did not hear whatever bothered Christie.

"Mommie, are you going somewhere?" Toby asked, bringing to everyone's attention the fact that his mother was half out of Satan's Throne, looking anxiously in the direction of the open doorway.

O'Flannery and Nadine shared a tension which Nadine didn't understand. When the shadow of their visitor crossed the doorway, O'Flannery reached out toward Nadine who automatically put her hand into his for a reasurrance she hadn't known she needed.

Marc Meridon hesitated politely in the doorway, but Nadine had an uncomfortable feeling that his dark eyes saw into her soul and were subtly amused at its goings-on.

"Pardon me. I was told that Mrs. Deeth had been seen walking on the temple path. I hope— Good evening, Christine. And Toby. You are Toby, of course." His smile for Christie Deeth was warm and attractive enough to impress even Nadine as he came into the room. There was obviously a strong feeling between him and Christie. While Nadine and O'Flannery made small talk, Marc went to Toby who looked at him with interest before remarking to his mother.

"He's nice. Not near as bad as Daddy said."

There was an embarrassed little hush before Marc laughed and they all followed suit, finding it more and more funny, to Toby's pink-cheeked delight. They all felt more at ease after that.

"We've now run out of cans," O'Flannery announced, handing the last one, a Screwdriver, to Marc who thanked him and promised not to ask for a refill.

Conversation became so general Nadine began to wonder if this wasn't the time to get a private word with Marc, to ask his advice about the grave-robbing she suspected of Dr. Haupt.

"Mr. Meridon," she began when she got a chance. "May I ask—?"

Toby sneezed.

His mother stared at him anxiously. "You aren't catching cold, dear?"

Toby sneezed again, insisting between sneezes

that he wasn't catching cold. Everyone took an interest, and volunteered a possible explanation. Nadine had the best idea.

"I wonder if Kinkajou is hiding in here somewhere. They do creep into the oddest places."

Everyone began to search while Toby sneezed. Eventually, Nadine got out an anti-histamine pill which helped the boy considerably.

They didn't find Kinkajou.

Nadine said, "I suppose the cat's been in here so much Toby can't help getting the scent of him."

"I imagine that must be it," Christie agreed, looking nervous. "It's about time we were going now. Would you mind awfully if I take the bottle of pills for Toby?"

"No, no. Please do."

Christie left soon after with Toby limping but insistent on using his own power, and with Marc Meridon taking his other hand.

On the portico between the pillars, Nadine and O'Flannery watched until the two adults and the boy dissolved in the blue twilight. Across the silent evening air a small sound came back to the pair on the steps. O'Flannery looked puzzled. "Did you hear that?"

"Just a sneeze. The boy is allergic."

"To what? Kinkajou is nowhere around."

She laughed cynically. "Don't be too sure. It's my opinion he could pop up anywhere. Either that or the boy is allergic to something—"

"I say again, to what?"

Nadine said, "Oh, come on in. Who cares?" She felt suddenly unsure of herself and of her thoughts.

177

TWELVE

Nadine relaxed that night, relying upon O'Flannery's enormous strength and that lazy, impudent look of his to keep her from depressing thoughts. They had a haphazard dinner off a rusting TV tray and spent the evening ransacking the temple for props to be used to incorporate some of the erotic and monetary fantasies of the Coven clients.

"Actually, I've noticed more clients want money. Or success, or power," Nadine remarked. "Sex isn't nearly as big a motive as it's cracked up to be."

"Some of them get what's promised. You can always take bows for that. Just a matter of using the contagious feel you have for success." He chucked her under the chin.

"No. It's more than that, Irish," she began seriously. "Does it ever occur to you that a lot of my predictions come true in a way that's far over my old percentage of correct guesses?"

"You're just getting better, Princess. Face it."

But he looked at her, almost studied her, several times during the evening, and she couldn't help doubting his easy assurance. She had not finished the thought that her question prompted: "Am I getting help of some kind in order to make those predictions and promises come true?" Was there some electric impulse she had struck on that put the words in her mouth? No use in saying that aloud. He *would* think she had lost her mind!

Instead of returning to the Spa for the night, she and O'Flannery brought a load of pillows out to the cool portico and slept there.

The occasional Pacific breeze that got across the barrier of the Sentinel Rocks made the air faintly salty and helped Nadine to sleep, but very early in the morning the wind died down. Either the still, warm air or her own bad conscience roused her in confusion from a nightmare that frightened her even when the details were obscure. She sat up, leaning back on her elbows, wondering what had aroused her. It was that time after night had gone but before sunrise when the whole world of the valley lay below her, pleasantly relieved of the day's pressures.

If I could say the same! she thought, and then became aware that Irish was both awake and staring at her. She scowled at him crossly.

"You know I don't like being watched."

"Then, Me Darlin', don't be talking in your sleep about cats and dead bodies and ashes."

She shot him a quick glance. "Did I really? I wonder why?"

"Don't play the innocent with me. I know you too well. And if you're going to lie to me about it, then keep that pretty mouth shut while you sleep. You never know who may be listening."

She sat up stiffly. "To coin a phrase, what's that supposed to mean? Are you afraid somebody's bugged the place?"

"No, Princess. But there's got to be something

that makes you so scared. Why do you keep looking over your shoulder and mine? You must be expecting somebody."

"At this hour? Don't be ridiculous. That is," the light of another warm day was beginning to open up the mountain peaks, and she made a sweeping gesture toward them. "I sometimes feel that scenery itself is watching us."

He settled himself again on his pillow. "You've had it! And for God's sake, stop dreaming! You interrupt my beauty sleep.'

"Yes, Master!" But it wasn't quite that simple. After gazing thoughtfully at the line of dawn above the rugged eastern slopes, Nadine murmured, "What did you mean yesterday when you were talking about grave-robbings?"

He turned and stared at her. She was several feet away and didn't at first realize why he was so silent. She thought he must have fallen asleep again, but he said abruptly, "What about it? Is that your next step—buying up stolen bodies for the ceremonies?"

"You really are the most offensive creature! No, to answer you, I didn't intend to use them. But what would you think if you saw a sealed urn with the name of somebody you knew was dead? Somebody famous?"

"You *have* bought up something! Are you crazy? You show that in the ceremony and you'll have the whole county invading this place. And let me tell you, the owners of the Cove may be very unpleasant to you about it."

So there was no help from O'Flannery for her problem. She must do as she had originally intended, rely upon Marc Meridon. She pretended to forget all about it, asking Irish, apropos of his advice, "Have you heard anything more about the ownership since we were in San Francisco?"

He considered. "Meridon's in it, and that's as far as I can get. Friend Haupt is strictly one of the minor players. You saw how he backed down to Meridon the other day, letting you go. You've nothing to worry about from the Hot Springs Führer."

"That's what you think." But she didn't explain. She had made up her mind that Marc Meridon was still the only person she could speak to about her suspicions of Haupt and his gang.

She both dreaded and looked forward to the truth. Curiosity had served her well all her life, even when the results were painful, but the pressures of her doubts built up that hot, sunny morning to such an extent that she felt she couldn't get down to the Spa fast enough. Her anxiety to see Meridon was difficult to explain to O'Flannery; so she merely complained that she was devastatingly hungry for a good brunch. O'Flannery appeared to accept this, but there was no doubt he suspected her of something nefarious.

They went briskly down the mountain trail in the morning sunlight, but when Nadine made a tentative gesturn of reconciliation, slipping her arm around O'Flannery's waist, he did nothing to return her affection. It was in a very uncertain mental and emotional state that she got through breakfast that morning for which she had no real appetite.

It shouldn't be too surprising therefore, when Nadine excused herself to Irish on the grounds of business, but with the intention of going to find Meridon.

"Then you intend to hold a service tonight?" he wanted to know, suddenly as alert as a cat at a mousehole. "You pull something tonight, Kid, and that's the end of it for me!"

She had for some weeks slated a service for this night, but apparently he had forgotten. "Why shouldn't I hold one? We've got Buddy Hemplemeier on edge, and that violinist, Illich, practically offered me the shirt off his back for a kind word from his young friend. Now is the time to take advantage of all this eagerness to get rid of their money."

He shrugged. "Well, if that's all it is. Meanwhile, suppose I go and get Illich's boyfriend to play ball."

In a slightly better humor with each other, they left the Spa's dining room, Nadine reminding him, "Be careful that one of those gay boys doesn't snap you up. You'd be a great temptation to them."

He laughed and they parted. She waited until he had gone and then she went into the Reception Office. Caro Teague, in an unattractive black, mini-dress, was working on Spa's books. It always amused Nadine to see how the Spa played up the romanticism of the place; for the ballpoint pen on the delicate kidney-shaped desk was pink. So was the set of cards signed by new clients. It came as something of a letdown that the double-entry ledger Caro was working with was a prosaic black with red reinforced corners.

"Have you seen Mr. Meridon this morning?" Nadine asked, when a throat-clearing produced no reaction from Caro.

The girl looked up blankly. It was incredible to Nadine that anyone could have cared so much about that wretched Ricardo Shahnaz, but the girl did more than care for him. As she made all too clear now, she held Nadine somehow responsible.

"Not since very early, Miss Janos."

Nadine could have kicked herself for the quick apology she made. "I'm so sorry about your . . . friend. He was very sick when I met him at the blue-green pool. Ulcers, he said. But of course, there must have been complications of—"

"It *was* ulcers, and *only* ulcers!" the girl flashed. "He never had a thing wrong with his heart. It's you that killed him. You and—someone else."

Nadine felt a sharp twist of fear. "Me and who?"

"I don't know. But I'll find out. You with your evil temple! Your precious devils! You used one of them, somehow, to kill Ricardo. He wasn't sick. Not that sick!"

"But why? What would I gain by killing that greasy gigolo? Why?" Nadine was genuinely bewildered.

Caro threw the bookkeeping pen at her. "Because he wouldn't give you a tumble. That's why! An ugly, rotten phoney like you—No wonder!"

Nadine walked out of the room, trying not to act either hurried or nervous. It took a bit of doing. She had begun to think of Dr. Haupt, and of the swiftness with which he had cremated the unfortunate Shahnaz. Still, she had no reason to believe the girl was right. Shahnaz was sick enough in that blue-green pool. But was he dying at that minute? Marc Meridon said he was, and she did not like to go against that formidable man.

Meanwhile, where to find him? She thought of all the people in the Spa who might know. The most logical, naturally, was Christie Deeth. She went to the pink salon phone and called Christie's suite. The chambermaid answered. Mrs. Deeth was out with her son. Young Toby took a fancy to go swimming and she had taken him up to the Hot Springs since the blue-green pool was not therapeutic.

"Rather she than I," Nadine remarked and punctuated this with a whistle. The blue-green pool might not be therapeutic but she trusted it fully as much as the Hot Springs pool, in spite of Ricardo Shahnaz' recent demise.

The chambermaid muttered "Balmy!" and cut off the connection.

After a moment's thought Nadine remembered the Mirror Bar where she had several times seen Meridon. She didn't personally like the place with its Specialty-of-the-House cocktails. Rumor said the added ingredients in various drinks were Speed, Acid, and a dozen other "mind-broadening" drugs. It might all be just talk but Nadine was much too proud of the size of her own mind to allow for any broadening.

Because she was uneasy in her memory of the pool, she walked past with deliberation. A wealthy teen-age singer and his latest girl friend were beating the waters about and their screaming echoes bounced off the curved roof in an eerie reminder of poor Shahnaz' voice two nights ago. She left them to their splashings and went on through the hall into the Mirror Bar. It was deserted, an unusual condition, and even more unusual, the handsome young barman was away from his post. It was not like the Spa to overlook any chance of catering to its spoiled clients.

She went in, took a good look, and finding nothing but her own face endlessly reflected, was about to leave when Marc Meridon came in. He looked a little surprised at seeing her, but fortunately for her pride, he did not seem displeased.

"Ah, good morning, Miss Janos. Has our barman let you down? Shall I get you something?"

"No, thank you. That is, it's too early in the day."

He went over to the bar. "I was to meet someone, but I seem to be early." She wondered if he was to meet Christie here. If so, he wouldn't want Nadine hanging around. He went on. "The least I can do is return your hospitality of last night. I take it you don't want one of the Specials."

She looked up with suspicion, but his smile was perfectly innocent, almost as innocent as Toby's. She managed to keep her equilibrium which wasn't easy in his company.

She said, "In my profession, I have to keep my head. But do have your own drink. Don't let me stop you."

She noticed that he didn't drink, however.

Whether it was one of his idiocyncrasies or just plain wisdom, she couldn't guess, but he never drank his own concoctions. No wonder he stayed thin. She felt that she had to soften this first awkwardness between them.

"I see some quinine water there at your elbow. May I have some?"

"Of course."

"And then, could I talk to you for a few minutes? I don't know anyone else who could advise me."

"By all means." He waved to the little glass table in the corner where she had sat with Christie the night Ricardo Shahnaz died.

She went and sat down with her back to the mirrored corner, hoping to avoid all those endless Nadine Janos faces. Much as she admired her own brain and ability, she was extremely critical of her physical appearance. Temporarily, however, she was distracted from endless visions of her exterior self, by the slim dark shadow of Marc Meridon who sat down facing her, studying her with flattering attention.

To a woman who always had her emotions well under control, he was disconcerting. He had done nothing. He hadn't touched her or used any of the usual ploys, but she felt the enormous attraction of the man, and couldn't help envying Christie Deeth, who received the benefit of those sombre dark eyes, shadowed as they were by long lashes. Nadine thought curiously, they were shadowed as if to hide the burning passion within. Lucky Christie Deeth!

Marc set the highball glass across the table in front of her, the ice cubes rattling loudly in the silence of the room. With an uncertainty and lack of self-confidence that was most unfamiliar to her, she toyed with the glass, sipped a little, deeply aware of his gaze.

"It is about something I saw yesterday in those Tudor houses facing the street." He looked politely interested, no more. She went on more rapidly. "It really began when I decided to take your advice and accept Dr. Haupt's aid at the temple."

"My advice? Surely not. Was that precisely my advice? I don't remember."

She bit her lower lip. He was clearly a stickler for detailed facts. "Maybe not. But I understood you to suggest that I go out and listen to the comments of my Coven members, and act accordingly."

He nodded, his eyebrow slightly raised. "That seems more nearly to fit the case. And then?"

"Then, after hearing what a smash he was at the Coven, I went to find him and he was gone. But I overheard some very odd bits of conversation. All about paying ghouls and so forth."

"I see. And you leaped instantly to the conclusion that these were literally ghouls."

She was annoyed at the way he had of putting her down, but when she heard his reminder it did sound as though she had jumped to several conclusions. She flashed a wide, if reluctant, smile. "Precisely. Several remarks added to the general picture. At any rate, when I left that awful place—"

"Awful?"

She ignored the teasing note. "I had to cross a field or two to get back to the street. And guess what I found behind one of those empty Tudor fronts."

"A live ghoul?"

She laughed into her glass, spilling drops of quinine water. She was more nervous than ever, and wondered why. "Worse. Someone's ashes."

"Someone's? Now you do surprise me. May I ask how you single out ashes in order to identify them as belonging to a human being?"

"By the little name plate that had fallen off," she said in triumph. She became aware of distant sounds from the pool, from the parking lot behind the Spa, even footsteps inside the building, in the distance. All marked the contrasting quiet in this room. She prompted him. "Doesn't that make sense?" But by now she was aware of what really had troubled her during the whole interview.

He knew about the ashes! He had known all along.

She was so dumbfounded she could think of no way to get out of this awkward impasse. "I— I think I must have made too much out of it. It may have a totally different explanation." He did not help her by giving her any indication of his own thoughts, and she went on scrambling, recognizing the cowardice and ambition that made her afraid to disagree with him. "I suppose it could be a joke. I thought the thing was a common jar or vase, at first. Yes. That would be like Haupt's weird sense of humor." She got up, not wanting any more to do with the subject. She especially didn't want to get in trouble with the owner of the Lucifer Cove Spa. He could ruin her.

"Yes," he agreed. "I think you've guessed it. I know Dr. Haupt has a perverted sense of humor, and he made some jokes recently about using ashes from the ovens for certain erotic thrills in his little night entertainments. I doubt if anyone took him seriously. But they are only ashes, Miss Janos. Bear that in mind. Common ashes from the ovens below the Clinic."

He walked to the door with her, thanked her for her information in a voice so sincere she could appreciate his ability to dissemble. He went back into the Mirror Bar when she left him. Walking toward her along the tile past the pool was Dr. Haupt. He greeted her in his harsh gutteral voice, and went on. When she had passed the pool with its laughing, splashing swimmers, she looked back. To settle any of her remaining doubts, the doctor stepped into the Mirror Bar. So this was the person Marc Meridon had gone to the bar to meet! She felt she needed no more proof.

It was terrifying in its significance. "One of these days I've got to leave the Cove. Next month. Or the month after, for certain."

Meanwhile, there was a Coven Ceremony tonight. She went up to her suite, wrote out a brief pattern of the night's ceremony including the various "specials." She had no doubt the newcomers would be disappointed when they came, expecting another "Hitler" to pop out of the flames of hell, but it couldn't be helped. Dr. Haupt was not going to repeat that unsavory trick. It threw everything out of joint.

Late in the afternoon O'Flannery joined her, with several large contributions, and a promise from Sergi Illich's young muscleboy to meet Illich at the temple.

"The kid says he'll meet the violinist tonight and make up the quarrel if Illich is reasonable. I have my doubts entirely."

"Never mind. It's the best we can do." She gathered up her props. "I wish you'd worked it so they can really make it up. It would help our image."

O'Flannery stopped in the act of taking her load from her. "You just pull something tonight, Princess," he said in a voice she had never heard before, "and you've seen the last of me."

"Irish! For heaven's sake, don't you turn against me. I'm so nervous now!"

But when he asked why, she didn't dare to tell him about the urn or the talk of ghouls, or what she suspected of Dr. Haupt. She saw O'Flannery watching her frequently during dinner and afterward, as she dressed for the service. Usually, he was concerned for her success when the weather was bad, and in the late afternoon heat lightning began to follow a hot weather shower. But he ignored it as Nadine tried to. Summer storms did not lately keep the clients away.

Tonight Nadine would be entirely in black, with a sequinned headpiece shaped like a Babylonian ziggurat, with layers rising to the high, squared crown. This covered all of her hair, making her face whiter, more transparent by contrast, and her eyes hypnotic lights inside that frame of darkness. When the alter girl showed up, a pretty, youngish sylph with lanky dark hair carefully streaked to shades of brown and yellow, she ruined Nadine's evening by remarking in wide-eyed innocence.

"You look marvy close up, Ma'am. Not near as old as I thought."

Nadine snapped her eyes at O'Flannery significantly.

"Get her out of here!"

To make matters worse, O'Flannery laughed, but he got the girl out of Nadine's dressing room. Left alone, Nadine stood perfectly still for a few minutes, taking deep breaths to ward off the stage-fright that briefly paralyzed her before every performance as the priestess to My Lord Satan. The world with its heavy rain squall and the rumble of thunder drifted away from her temporarily. She concentrated on her carefully planned movements in the ceremony. In the silence that followed her concentration was interrupted by the memory of that curious presence in this room before the last ceremony.

When the sounds reached her of the Coven's commandment chant with its childish blasphemy punctuated by distant chains of heat lightning, she knew no other world presence shared this space with her, and in considerable relief she left the room, striding slowly along the hall to the open door behind the altar dais. Her pulse beat rapidly. She was keyed up, but this was usually a help, rather than a hindrance. Like an actress she had learned to seem real but always to remain in control of the part she played.

On her way to the dais, however, she heard voices in the prop room and her concentration was ruined. She stuck her head in. Sergi Illich's muscleboy friend was playing hard to get, and the violinist, looking parchment-thin, had turned away, apparently defeated. Really, he'd be better off dead than in this zombie condition.

What a tiresome pair! Anything to ruin her performance!

"Gentlemen, please! The ceremonies are beginning. Take your places in the nave. We must have no disturbance to distract My Lord Satan." It was extremely annoying to hear the muscleboy's laugh grate on her ears.

"Yeah. Mustn't louse up your act, Lady Macbeth."

Illich drifted by Nadine on his way out and remembering his contribution to the temple, she called after him. "You will find our thoughts united for you, sir. Don't despair!"

The muscleboy stared at her, grinning unpleasantly. "You really are a pompous witch, Lady Macbeth."

"You—you clod!" She stalked out indignantly.

It was this encounter undoubtedly that threw off her timing. She made her entrance onto the dais much too rapidly, with draperies flying, and a total lack of that frightening calm, the alabaster mask, the feel of an unearthly otherworld about her. They had drawn a good crowd tonight, although the meeting was earlier than usual; for she had hoped, vainly, to beat the storm. Probably the crowd was due in great part to Dr. Haupt's silly trick the other night. The faithful had hiked up to the temple in spite of the rain, and she regretted her own failure to create a memorable entrance.

It did not help that just as she raised her arms to call upon My Lord Satan, she caught sight of

Erich Haupt standing at one side of the auditorium, grinning, his black peaked hood raised so there could be no mistake in his identity. At least, tonight, he had not played up his physical resemblance, but all the same, his evil smile annoyed her. As she looked away, the violinist's muscleboy joined Haupt, and she felt the vibrations of their joint disbelief in her. It was a bad omen for her success.

Across the nave O'Flannery had seen the pair and was watching them. Thank heaven for that!

The ritual went on. Possibly the Coven didn't even know how unsure of herself she felt tonight. Constant repetition had made her almost letter perfect. When she looked down at the space below the dais where the blasphemous Communion was taken, a man in robe and hood knelt before her and before the altar with its inverted cross. This had several times happened before when someone, usually a woman, wanted a special favor and knelt as if propitiating the All-Powerful. This man had his hands hidden in his robes and he looked frail, as if his legs had given away under him. She guessed it might be Sergei Illich and when the special prayers came, she pointedly called on My Lord Satan to bring happiness "to one who supplicates you, having lived in your service and denied all ties to the weaker gods. He has long offered his soul to your godhead and is your child, beseeching you."

That, at least, ought to calm the unfortunate Illich.

The summer storm had moved overhead and a lightning bolt struck the mountainside between the temple and the valley. Nadine's congregation shuddered as one. Nadine, too, had felt the shock but hid its effect in her floating black draperies, telling herself nothing could better serve her performance. She made several prayers for good contributors, pleased at the proper lighting effects around the inverted crucifix.

The latest lightning bolt had struck near the power lines and the indirect neon lights dimmed, leaving only the trick lights, the oil lamps and candles to create their illusions. When the last neon lights went out, there was a concerted gasp from the congregation but this was almost immediately absorbed by the wild roll of thunder overhead. A sound so great in the flickering half-dark it appeared to come from the nave itself where Sergei Illich knelt.

Nadine raised her arms once more. She thought she must have pulled a muscle when her fingertips began to prickle. . . . Don't tell me they're going to sleep now! What's the matter with me? She shifted her feet, nervously aware that a numbness was creeping over her toes as well. The echo of the thunder still remained on the air when she recalled the last time she felt this curious numbness, and she stared down into the narrow space below the dais. The kneeling man in the hood and robe had fallen forward and was still. O'Flannery was making his way toward the man's motionless body, but Nadine found it impossible to move. She knew what she would find. The body of Sergei Illich, just as she had foreseen it the afternoon she crossed the dry creek bridge.

I wished it on him. I did it, as I wished poor Irena Byaglu out of my hair!

She forced herself to move, painfully raised her arms, calling upon My Lord Satan to "bless this Coven of your worshipers as they depart, carrying with them their devotion to you, body and soul." It was the only thing she could think of to get rid of the crowd before they learned what O'Flannery was about to uncover. But though many of the congregation turned and faced the aisles obediently, too many of them began to edge toward the altar, their eyes gleaming with curiosity, framed by the masking black hoods.

Damn! she thought ... What will I do? They won't hold still for this a genuine death in their midst. None of the phoney stuff.

Suddenly, as if in answer to her unspoken prayer, the pushing forward stopped. Those in the lead fell back. There were scattered gasps. A scream. And without cause. Even O'Flannery stopped in mid-step and stared up at her. His mouth had fallen open.

Belatedly, she realized they were not looking at her but up, higher, at the altar behind her. She found herself turning in the most gingerly way, to peer over her shoulder.

It was there in mid-air, the obscure and terrible thing she had seen that first night after her return from San Francisco. The vagueness, the aura like a fiery haze, and in its midst, the eyes burning from their core of flame...

Nadine told herself passionately, "I'm not insane! They have all seen it. I called upon him and he answered me. I have the power. I really have the power."

She was torn between her first terror and the wild boost to her ego. Even as she stared, the terrible image faded until nothing remained but the upturned crucifix, and the eyes, shorn of their halo of fire. Just the second before they vanished, she thought she recognized the sombre, luminous quality of someone she knew well. But she found her usually active brain numbed by the horror of those last few seconds.

Try to think! Whose eyes?

It was wiped out of her mind as if by magic, whatever haunting memory had warned her. She groped for the altar, held on tight until her head cleared. Immediately below the dais, O'Flannery knelt over the black-clad bundle. She saw him raise the man's hood. The still, pale eyes of Sergei Illich were revealed, as she had expected. O'Flannery wrested the gun out of the suicide's fingers. But he said nothing, nor did he uncover the rest of the face.

O'Flannery waited until the trembling, buzzing crowd had filed out. After the Hitler-type apparition two nights ago, they were less impressed than Nadine by the ghastly thing they had seen.

She had an hysterical impulse to laugh. They gave her greater credit than she deserved. They thought it was she who had produced My Lord Satan. She, who was more genuinely terrified than any of them!

THIRTEEN

Another hellish hour followed for Nadine and O'Flannery. O'Flannery couldn't persuade anyone either to get help from the County Sheriff's office or to help him move the violinist's body to the Clinic for the autopsy, so the unpleasant business of helping him get Illich ready was left to the badly shaken Nadine. Between them, she and O'Flannery examined Illich whose single bullet had shattered the base of his skull. Staring at what remained of the sensitive, intellectual face, Nadine had an awful fear she would be sick, but was shaken out of it by O'Flannery's furious command, "Behave yourself, or I'll be at you!"

"B-but a Coroner! The police. They'll ask why we moved it."

"Since when have the police meddled in here? Don't be daft, Girl."

Then, with an effort of will they wrapped the body in two of her bed sheets and the Irishman lifted the corpse in its temporary shroud.

"I'll report it. Can you carry it alone?" she asked, knowing he could, and would, but wishing they needn't give over the poor body to Dr. Haupt's tender concern. Even the violinist's great love had departed earlier with the rest of the Coven.

"Sure," said Irish, without looking at her. "You'll be having me lose faith in my muscles. And they're all that's of use to me these days. Serving the hounds of hell; that's me!"

"What!"

"Open the door."

She did so, still staring at him. "You're not blaming me for his death! I tried to help him. It's not my faith." But of course it was. She had foreseen this death at the bridge yesterday, and the knowledge was like looking at her own death. A horror! Where had she gotten the power? She would have prayed to be relieved of it, if she believed in any gods.

"Get out of my way. Your new partner, the Führer of the Cove, will be wondering where I've gone with the latest fuel for his little potbellied stove."

"Don't say that. You know I have no use for Haupt."

He stepped out onto the portico steps, shifting his load and looking up at the sky. The storm had moved on. Following him, Nadine could see the wiry streaks of summer lightning over the distant mountain peaks. She tried again to get him over what was obviously a harder than usual Gaelic sulk.

"Look, Irish . . . Honey, I had nothing whatever to do with what happened tonight. I swear I didn't!" What was the matter with him? He didn't lose his temper, or swear, or get drunk. She had a depressing notion that things were really different between them.

He looked at her and she was shocked at the

cold dislike in that look. "It's not like you to whine. Night, Princess."

Stupified, she watched him go and belatedly screamed after him, "I never whine!" but she wasn't sure he heard her. Or cared, if he did hear.

For the first time in her memory, she didn't know what to do. She knew that, both financially and in personal reputation, she had never been so successful. Half of Lucifer Cove believed tonight that she could produce that highly convincing devil's apparition out of a few lights, some dummy curtain effects and maybe a mirror or two. And all the time the insufferable Dr. Haupt had watched the ceremony, probably guessing he would inherit Sergei Illich's body, and thinking he was going to be her partner.

"Not while I live and breathe! He'll never have one inch of this place."

By now, with O'Flannery's loss, she was shaken out of her panic and indecision. It was still fairly early. The storm had passed and the valley was still shrouded in blue twilight. At the north end she could see the Hot Springs gaily lighted, with a string of little blue-haloed gloves outlining the heated pool where therapeutic swimming still went on. Locking the temple whose altar looked harmless and unhaunted now, she walked down to the Spa, unaware that though the headdress had long since fallen off, she still fluttered her black draperies around her. Those who saw her supposed the costume was a deliberate advertising of her post as priestess to the devil.

The big-boned female receptionist from the

Hot Springs met her as she came out of her room in one of her stark black and white chongsams, split to the hip to accommodate her rapid stride.

"Good evening, Miss Janos. Congratulations upon your business merger. It should give you and the good doctor practically control of the Cove, north and south."

Nadine stiffened, her dread quickly turning to anger. "What do you mean by that?"

But the woman smirked knowingly. "Have I been naughty and let the cat out? It's being so much talked about."

"Where?" Nadine was breathing fire.

"For one thing, at the Hot Springs. At the barbecue around the outside pool. There's quite a crowd enjoying the party. Everyone says so, including Dr. Haupt. He came past here almost an hour ago, calling in some night workers. They're expecting poor old Illich's body, as you know. You're marvelous, Miss Janos. You hexed that whole crowd tonight."

Nadine said furiously. "That's not all I'm going to hex!" and hurried up the street, toward the Hot Springs.

The Old Witch, Mrs. Peasecod, who owned the Notions Shop, was in the process of closing a deal with the door open, while she discussed the ordering of a puppy by Christie Deeth. Seeing Nadine, one of her best customers for the properties of the communion wine and other trifles, the Old Witch called to her.

"You there, Unholy One! What do you think of the treachery of this lovely creature? She asks for dogs. I tell her this is a place for cats. And what will Kinkajou say to those beastly enemies on his property, eh?"

Nadine stopped briefly to get her breath. To Christie whose greeting was restrained as always with her, she said, "I suppose the dog is for your little boy. How is he? Do you think the valley is going to be good for him?"

Christie shrugged. "I can't say, as yet. We hope so, Marc and I. There seem to be some allergies we have to consider. Toby, of course, loves it all. I can hardly get him out of that Hot Springs pool. He's not used to the buoyant warm water. I'd better finish this order and get back to him. He should be in bed at this hour."

Mrs. Peasecod smiled unctiously, "Exactly so. You will read and sign the order? We do not have many animals at the Cove. Not . . ." She giggled, "not of the kind you are buying. But naturally, we make every effort to please our largest stockholder, Mr. Meridon."

"Naturally," Christie repeated with a certain ironic twist to the word.

Nadine went on in a hurry, figuring that if Christie, also on her way to the Hot Springs, caught up with her it would be awkward all around. They were always uncomfortable in each other's company. As for Nadine's own motive for the angry visit, she knew herself well enough to understand that this passion to see Dr. Haupt was purely selfish. It concerned her own life's work whose rewards she refused to share. Let Haupt dig up his own "tricks."

Whatever apparition had appeared to her and to her congregation, she reasoned after an hour's puzzlement, must be explained by coincidence, mass hypnotism, or just the luck of her profession. She didn't know yet whether it was to be good luck or bad, but she had seen and studied too many tricks in her life to fall completely under an illusion of the supernatural.

She reached the big Hot Springs wire fence and walked a little way to the gates which were wide open invitingly. One of the Hot Springs messengers, a devastatingly handsome young fellow in a kind of flesh-colored jock-strap, met her. Behind him she could see the crowd around the pool, many of them teen-agers only a few years older than Toby, though far more sophisticated. Caro Teague, in a dark terry-cloth poncho that revealed her lame left leg along with the beautifully proportioned right leg, was watching over Toby. He clung to the pool's tile side near her and kicked out his feet behind him in some kind of therapy session.

The Hot Springs messenger saw Nadine's careful survey of those at the pool and asked if she would like to join them. "Or have you come to see Dr. Haupt. I'm afraid he's in the Clinic. An emergency came up."

"I quite understand. Just tell me what color to follow. I'll find him."

He winked. "In this case, I think it couldn't be anything but the corridor marked in black, could it?"

"Not if Erich Haupt has anything to do with it. I'll find it myself. Please don't bother."

"Of course. Only—" A teen-aged blonde girl at the pool called him and he waved. "Be right there. I'll take you to Reception, Miss Janos."

She said impatiently, "Don't bother. I know my way that far, at least."

He made gestures, pointing, reminding her of the second turn and numerous other advice which she ignored. She didn't want them ganging up on her. As she started along the marigold path to the labyrinthine building, the young Hot Springs employee raced over toward the poolside. He was paying no more attention to her. Good! She didn't want any more "guided tours." She had just entered the building when she heard light, uneven footsteps behind her, limping over the tile floor. It was young Toby Deeth, dripping wet and breathless.

"Toby! You shouldn't be here. Does Miss Teague know where you are?"

He clung to her to rest his weakened leg and get his breath, but nothing destroyed his eagerness.

"You own Kinkajou; don't you?"

She couldn't help smiling at him in spite of her bad temper and the shadow of the night's events which refused to go away. "Nobody owns Kinkajou. He belongs to the Cove."

"Me too?"

"You too. But you mustn't be in here. I'm going to a place where dead—where sick people are. You be a good boy and go back to Miss Teague. She will be worried." She walked on, hearing the hare click of her heels echoed at a slight distance by the slap and drag of Toby's feet.

"Please let me go too. Caro said Kinky always comes back to you. She doesn't like cats, Caro doesn't. She said cats are creepy. But not Kinky. Could I go after you where Kinkajou is? Caro said—"

She stopped again, took him by one thin, wet shoulder. She had an entirely uncharacteristic fear for him, that he would see what went on in this place, that he would—somewhere, sometime —understand it.

"No, Toby. I don't know where the cat is. Your mother is going to get you a puppy. She is ordering it now. If you don't go back out to the pool, she will be anxious about you. You don't want to worry your mother, do you?"

He tugged on her sleeve ingratiatingly. "Mommy wants me to feel good. She said so. I feel good if Kinky comes."

"You sneeze."

"That's okay." He kept following her and had just reached a branching corridor, one way marked in pink, which would take her to the black marks and what she thought of as the Disposal Area. Above all, she didn't want this boy with his beautifully trusting face to see the rotting heart of this place. With a quick, frantic twist, she forced his fingers off her sleeve. He winced, and when she said severely, "Go on, now! Back to the pool!" he stood there staring at her with an expression that cut her to the quick. It was like a trusting animal who had been kicked. She forced herself to hurry around the corner of the hall where she waited a minute or two, but he had apparently given up. His small, dragging footsteps retreated very slowly.

The whole incident roused her to a fresh anger against Erich Haupt. After all, she reasoned, if it hadn't been for his bold-as-brass assumption of a partnership with her, and if he hadn't developed the ghastly business with his human disposal section, she wouldn't be forced to wander through this hellish place, or to be cruel to a crippled child.

"It's not my fault. Not at all! I didn't want any of this." She repeated this so often in the next few minutes that she finally convinced herself. But it was a struggle.

There were lights on in the plush Women's Exercise Room and hysterical giggles from someone. She hurried past trying to remember exactly where the black-marked turnoff to the Disposal Area began. The corridor turned its direction several times. Once, hearing slight noises behind her, she swung around, listened and saw nothing. The lighting was dimmed to a dull, depressing blue at this hour. She shivered, turned another corner and quite suddenly came to a black-marked corridor.

In the distance a door stood open wide. There was a lot of noisy activity inside. It was the laboratory and the huge incinerator beyond. She had come this far and found herself shaking, no longer with anger but with a deathly fear. So much for her courage, the bold confrontation she intended with Dr. Haupt. She drew herself up, bolstered her flagging bravery with a reminder that Haupt needed her too much to get rid of her tonight.

Nevertheless, when the light from that doorway ahead of her darkened briefly, and Dr. Haupt's white uniformed figure strode out into the hall and faced her with the lascivious and thoroughly false smile she recalled so well, she almost turned and ran.

"Good evening again, Miss Janos. A happy augury for the future, this meeting. You did come to consolidate our little partnership?"

She walked toward him. The normal, even quality of her voice surprised her. "On the contrary, Doctor. I am here for quite a different reason. And the others, who agree with me, are to meet us here." It was a lie but unless he was a mind-reader he needn't know that. "We feel that Sergei Illich's body should be taken to the County Seat for the autopsy."

He glanced behind him, into the laboratory and that hungry, flaming mouth in the room beyond. "Since that would entail a great deal of red tape, I am sure you will be glad to hear that it is no longer necessary. The poor fellow's physical condition made a delay highly improper. Fortunately, we are well equipped to handle such matters here."

"No, Doctor, I'm afraid not. They don't agree with you." *They!* That illusive and mysterious *they*. She hoped the implied pressure would work with him. She added, to protect herself, "I came ahead hoping to get to you before they do. To—to warn you."

He still seemed suspicious, but not quite so sure of himself as they reached the open doorway. She controlled a shudder and remarked brightly, "How handy! Very antiseptic, too. No wonder you like to handle the whole business yourself. From cradle to the grave, you might say." She avoided the blank, emotionless eyes of the two men in hospital whites with butcher aprons who were behaving very much as they had earlier when she watched them at their sinister work. They ignored her and curiously enough, ignored Dr. Haupt as well.

He pointed out various aspects of the laboratory which had little to mark it as more sinister than most. She could see his white-clad figure vividly reflected in the glass of the nearest instrument cabinet, with her own face blurred and pale beside him.

"And you may see how quickly we rid ourselves of danger from the many contaminations which might cause problems. The incinerator just beyond." He waved toward that area with what sounded to her like genuine pride. He was the most horrible, she thought, because he believed in all this god-like destruction of human beings.

They seemed to have utilized the underground, sulphurous heat in some way because she could smell the sulphur now, a sickening breath-catching stench, and she avoided that end of the circular disposal room where pipes carried up the heat and the smell was greatest. On a plinth just inside the disposal room lay a covered object which she suspected was Sergei Illich. One of the two expressionless men working here, opened the great central furnace which belched out flame. He stoked the white-hot mass within from a distance of several feet. The other workman went over to the whitecovered bundle on the plinth.

Nadine cried, "No, don't! Not until other doctors have examined him." When Dr. Haupt looked at her, surprised and slyly amused, she added the only thing she could think of "Mr. Meridon told me he has changed his mind."

"Ah!" It was obvious this stopped him briefly. He looked around. Both workers were lifting the covered body on what appeared to be stretcher poles painted black—some's macabre sense of humor, probably—and they started across to the open maw of the incinerator.

Nadine took several rapid steps toward them, stopped by the barrier of the doctor's arm.

"Too late, I am afraid. Better that we keep this among ourselves. A few experiments on the body, understand. All consciousness was gone. He never knew. And now you present a problem yourself. A pity. You and I would have been well-suited as partners."

She pretended desperately not to understand this threat.

"Wait until morning. You don't want to arouse suspicious that you are doing something they wouldn't approve of." She saw that he was uncertain, half convinced by her mention of Marc Meridon who undoubtedly had a financial stake in this place.

In the few seconds that he hesitated, one of the workers made a hoarse, gutteral sound in his throat. He was staring at the doorway, his hands on the stretcher poles shaking so that the shrouded body slipped to one side of the stretcher. They all looked around.

Kinkajou had stalked into the disposal room, clearly regarding them with his usual contemptuous curiosity.

"It is only a cat!" Dr. Haupt exclaimed impatiently but the worker who had first given the alarm was backing to the incinerator's open door.

Nadine blessed the arrival of the cat which probably had saved her life, at least for the moment. Seeing the reaction of his laboratory worker and its contagion upon the other worker who had likewise begun to retreat in panic, Dr. Haupt left Nadine and took several angry strides toward the cat who naturally darted out of reach. Whatever the workers saw of danger in the cat, Dr. Haupt clearly was ignorant of it. He pursued Kinkajou now, thoroughly challenged and angry. Nadine, finding herself free, gave up all hope of saving the violinist's dead body, and started across to the doorway. She would still have to cross the laboratory once she got out of the disposal room, but thanks to Kinkajou, they were much too busy to stop her. She made it to the doorway, congratulating herself that she had kept in shape, and ran directly into Toby Deeth.

"He's here! I saw him! Here, Kitty . . . Kitty . . ." He was trying to squeeze past her. She reached out, sick with dread and anger at the silly, eager child, trying to hold onto him. It was a tussle and just as she had a tight grip on the squirming Toby, Dr. Haupt looked around.

"So! Another problem."

Toby took this opportunity to dash after Kinkajou, giggling at the ridiculous sight of the two men with their delicately balanced load, who panicked completely as the cat ran under the stretcher. Everything fell, and the first terrorized worker stumbled against the open incinerator door. The flames licked at his sleeve and with a frightful scream, he flung against the door banged shut and open with a resounding metal crash, showering the room with sparks.

Nadine was torn by two impulses. There was no longer any obstacle to her flight. The way out to the corridor with its black directional marks was perfectly free. But meanwhile, there was Toby, limping behind the incinerator, always missing the illusive Kinkajou. Nadine dove after the boy just as the world seemed to burst into fireworks. She caught Toby by the seat of his swim trunks, aware of frightful shrieks behind her, the ghastly stench of burning flesh and cloth, a scramble, and the slap of running feet.

"Kinky! Where's Kinky?" the boy cried as she dragged him across the floor.

Dr. Haupt, trying to smother the flames which had spread to the corpse on the floor flailed out as Nadine passed him dragging Toby. It was a fierce, crushing blow that caught her across the skull, reviving the sick headache that had pursued her the first day she woke up in the Hot Springs Clinic. She stumbled, picked herself up as Toby stopped struggling and turned to pull her along.

"He ran away. Kinky ran away. Quick! Everything's on fire."

"What a pair we are!" Nadine thought dizzily as they plunged toward the open door to the corridor. "A crippled boy and a knotheaded woman!" Then she screamed with pain as what felt like a sheet of flame flashed through the doorway and past her. The other of the workers. Seconds later, Dr. Haupt rushed past.

Nadine scrambled on with Toby. Behind them rolled the wild, rushing fury of the fire. Toby was slightly ahead of her, breathing in tight, hard sobbing gasps, dragging his leg but making speed. Suddenly he collapsed and Nadine fell on top of him. He was crying and she whispered, "Honey, I'm sorry. I couldn't help it."

"It's—it's a man." Toby had stumbled over what remained of one of the laboratory workers. He rolled off, moaning. "He's still on fire."

"I know. Come." She lifted him off and ran on, half carrying, half dragging him.

It was endless, this hellish corridor, with the pristine white walls eaten away inch by inch and foot by foot behind him. They should have run the other way, though Nadine was not sure which way they had come, the corridor was so full of smoke, and Toby's coughing at least, she supposed they had.

"Bend over," she ordered Toby. "Crunch as you breathe." There was a little help with the air this way, but then they saw ahead of them the open door of the Women's exercise room. In the doorway the second lab worker had fallen, and the lilac satin drapes swinging across the doorway had caught fire. They blazed wildly, fed by air from a duct somewhere, probably the airconditioning. Otherwise, the room was empty.

"I can't," whispered Toby, falling onto his knees.

"Yes, you can. Come on." She tried to lift him but found herself too weak. Weakness infuriated her. She dragged his dead weight a few inches, then saw it was useless. "You must. Your mother needs you."

"It's—it's all fire. I can't go that way."

She swung around frantically. The corridor ahead split in two directions. Both were full of smoke. "Not fire. Only smoke. Come!"

It was no use.

FOURTEEN

She dragged at his arms again.

He sneezed. She stared at him. He sneezed again. Then, miraculously, he began to raise himself, holding tight to her hands.

"He's here somewhere; isn't he?"

"Of course, he is. Kinky's leading us out," she insisted, not believing it.

"That way. He's that way."

She glanced from Toby to the left corridor, then dragged him along. The smoke thinned out almost at once, and they struggled on as Nadine recognized familiar marks along the wall. Toby sneezed again and giggled.

"Must be going the right way."

He was probably sneezing from all the smoke he had inhaled but she didn't contradict him. They turned a corner blindly and crashed into the arms of Marc Meridon. He lifted Toby to his shoulder and caught Nadine under her right arm. She never afterward remembered anything until she was hit by a delicious blast of fresh, evening air on the grounds as she saw O'Flannery running madly along the marigold path toward her.

With neat timing Meridon dropped her just as the Irishman caught her before she hit the gravel.

She muttered between long, painful breaths, "Please. Give me a second. Let me rest."

"Not here, Princess. Half the Hot Springs is tumbling down. The Fire Department's miles away. Quick!" But this time he picked her up easily and carried her to the buzzing, chattering crowd on the far side of the pool. When he put her down, she was able to see Marc Meridon approaching the crowd, looking only slightly dishevelled and flanked by the pallid, anxious Christie Deeth. She was caressing Toby's bare leg and repeatedly asking him now he felt. Between sneezes the boy insisted he was fine.

"And Kinkajou saved us. He showed us the way out. That's what made me sneeze."

Caro Teague had broken from the crowd, crying, and ran past Nadine to touch Toby and complain, "That hateful cat! Mrs. Deeth, it was the cat who made him run into that awful place."

"He led us out, didn't he, Priest Lady?" Toby insisted of Nadine.

Briefly distracted from the inferno in the distance, the crowd turned its attention to the feline argument. At the pause before Nadine answered, even Marc Meridon looked at her with a whimsical little smile that had its usual powerful effect upon her, as though they shared a delicious secret. Watching him carefully, to be certain he approved, she answered Toby.

"He did more than lead us out. He saved my life. I'm fairly sure Dr. Haupt would have killed me in that disposal room if Kinkajou hadn't popped in. He was—" She grinned at a thought. "He was providential, you might say."

214

Toby sneezed and insisted, "I said so, Mommy."

Someone started to call, "Where is the damned cat?" Someone else, mocking, yelled, "Here, Kitty," but then the Clinic side of the Hot Springs fell in upon itself with a great roar, throwing off a wide aura of sparks that reached nearly to the pool. Some of the onlookers began to run.

Meridon lifted Toby down to join his mother and Nadine said to him "Were there many lost in the fire?"

"So far as we can tell, only the two laboratory technicians."

Uneasily, she asked, "And Dr. Haupt?"

Marc glanced back at the smoke-stained reception room entrance. "He made it to the outside, but he died there on the lawn. Smoke inhalation, I imagine. Or simple heart failure. Does it matter? He had exhausted his usefulness."

Nadine gazed at him, open-mouthed. Mrs. Deeth had gone on to the gates with Toby and was wiping his nose after his sneezing spell. As Marc started to join her, Nadine caught his singed and smoke-stained sleeve, asking in a faint voice, "And me? Have I exhausted my usefulness?"

Meridon looked briefly surprised. Then he reached out, took her nervous, trembling hand in his cool fingers. "You? But you are my dearest ally. Now sleep well, Miss Janos. You did good work tonight."

He left her.

She was still shaking when O'Flannery hugged her to his warm, powerful body. "What was that all about, Princess?"

"I've no idea," she lied, but she could not stop shaking. "Honey, the fireworks are over. Let's go where it's warm."

He laughed, obviously taking this for a joke, and they walked out of the grounds together, past the oncoming fire engine and chief's car turning in through the gateway. "A little late," he remarked.

Nadine looked up at him. "Don't let it be too late, Irish. I need you."

His arm tightened its clasp around her tense shoulders. "That's all I've waited for, Princess. A lifetime or so, I think."

Somebody behind them complained, "They ought to give a medal to the cat they were talking about. Saved the kid. And the priestess too."

Someone else in Nadine's hearing said, "Where the devil did he go?"

"They're right about Kinkajou," Irish reminded Nadine. "Good little beast. Hope he wasn't caught in the collapse of the Clinic."

Nadine said before she thought. "Oh no. He's safe."

Because, of course, she knew Kinkajou had gotten out.